Books by Christopher Pike

BURY ME DEEP
CHAIN LETTER 2: THE ANCIENT EVIL
DIE SOFTLY
THE ETERNAL ENEMY
FALL INTO DARKNESS
FINAL FRIENDS #1: THE PARTY
FINAL FRIENDS #2: THE DANCE
FINAL FRIENDS #3: THE GRADUATION
GIMME A KISS
THE IMMORTAL
LAST ACT
THE LAST VAMPIRE
THE LAST VAMPIRE 2: BLACK BLOOD
MASTER OF MURDER
THE MIDNIGHT CLUB
MONSTER
REMEMBER ME
REMEMBER ME 2: THE RETURN
REMEMBER ME 3: THE LAST STORY
ROAD TO NOWHERE
SCAVENGER HUNT
SEE YOU LATER
SPELLBOUND
WHISPER OF DEATH
THE WICKED HEART
WITCH

Available from ARCHWAY Paperbacks

Christopher PIKE

Remember Me 3
THE LAST STORY

AN ARCHWAY HARDCOVER
Published by POCKET BOOKS
New York   London   Toronto   Sydney   Tokyo   Singapore

AN ARCHWAY HARDCOVER

 An Archway Hardcover published by
POCKET BOOKS, a division of Simon & Schuster Inc.
1230 Avenue of the Americas, New York, NY 10020

Library of Congress Catalog Card Number: 94-79698

ISBN: 0-671-87259-1

First Archway Hardcover printing February 1995

10 9 8 7 6 5 4 3 2 1

AN ARCHWAY HARDCOVER is a trademark of Simon &
Schuster Inc. The colophon is a registered trademark of
Simon & Schuster Inc.

Printed in the U.S.A.

For Marjorie

Remember Me 3
THE
LAST STORY

CHAPTER

I

*T*HE SILVER LINING of success often tarnishes before it can be enjoyed. For me, being rich and famous was both wonderful and awful. Wonderful because money and notoriety are necessary and useful in a world where almost everything can be purchased with them. Awful because that same wealth and fame caused me to forget that I can never truly own anything in this world. Like everyone else, I am here for only a short time and then, no matter how rich and important I have become, I will be gone. It's ironic that I, who have died and returned to life, should forget that. But forget it I did when I came face to face with my enemy.

Myself.

Shari Cooper. Jean Rodrigues. I have two names.

But perhaps I am being too hard on myself. After all, I was once a ghost who prayed only to be remembered. To have one more chance at life. And then, when that chance was miraculously granted, was it any wonder I should have run wild for a time? Yes, I can forgive myself, and hope those close to me can do the same. Because time *is* short.

Especially for me.

God, my head hurts. My heart aches.

Where to begin? Maybe at the beginning of the end. That would be a few days ago. My publisher had arranged a book signing for me at a large Barnes & Noble located in a California mall the size of Tokyo. The turnout was unexpected, even by my lofty standards. Two thousand young people showed up to have me scribble my name—my *real* name from my previous life, and now my pen name—on the inside cover of my latest best-seller. How young they seemed to me, although most were only a couple years short of my twenty-one years. Being famous does make you feel old and wise, like you know it all. Greeting each adoring fan with a quick smile and a flick of my pen, I felt like a queen.

"I'm your number-one fan," a cute redheaded girl said as she reached my table at the head of the line. She clutched a copy of *Remember Me*—my sixth book—to her chest, her eyes saucerlike and round. "I've read everything you've written."

"What's your name?" I asked, sticking out my hand for her copy of the book.

"Kattie. Is Shari Cooper a pen name, or is it your real name? I noticed you named the heroine of *Remember Me* Shari Cannon."

I glanced at Peter Nichols, in Lenny Mandez's body, sitting beside me, in his wheelchair. He smiled but didn't say anything. Peter enjoyed the signings more than I did. I didn't know why because all the attention was focused on me.

"It's real enough," I muttered. Taking the book, I opened it to the title page and scribbled: *For Kattie, Enjoy. Shari Cooper.* I don't use many different inscriptions inside my books. "Enjoy," "Best Wishes," "Be Good," and "Love and Kisses"—if the guy is cute that is. Actually, I didn't know what to say to people when they told me how great I was. Being a celebrity was fun but also confusing. Kattie lingered after I returned her book. The people behind her fidgeted. I had been signing for three hours straight and the line was still long. My right hand was numb. Kattie smiled shyly.

"I was just wondering," she asked, "where do you get your ideas?"

Had I been asked that question before? Once or twice, a million times. "I don't know," I said. "I really don't. They just come to me, at unexpected moments."

"But do you think you have a muse, like Sam O'Connor in that short story you wrote?"

I chuckled. Sam was a troll who lived in the closet. I said to Peter, "Do we have a troll in our closet?"

"There's only me," Peter said.

Kattie seemed confused. "Are you girlfriend and boyfriend?" she asked.

I hesitated, feeling Peter's eyes on me. "Yes. You look surprised, Kattie?"

She was not surprised, but embarrassed. "No. I just thought you were brother and sister." She shrugged. "I'm sorry."

"Don't be sorry," Peter said quickly. "We do look kind of alike."

Except for both of us being in Hispanic bodies, we looked nothing alike. My features were voluptuous, sensual. Since becoming a writing star, I had cut my hair short; my bangs brushed my eyes as they once did—in my earlier incarnation as Shari Cooper. Peter hadn't cut his straight black hair since he had wandered back in—he wore it long, down his back, in a ponytail I enjoyed tugging. Because he ate like a bird, he had become terribly thin, haggard even. Still, his dark eyes were bright and his smile seldom dimmed.

Like Peter, I understood Kattie's confusion. She saw me as a star, an idol, someone she dreamed of becoming. And here I was with a paraplegic. Knowing she'd never understand, I didn't try to explain. Plus anything I would have said would only hurt Peter's feelings.

"We've been through a lot together," I said to Kattie. "It's been great."

Kattie flashed me one last smile. "You're great." She held up *Remember Me.* "I've already read this new book three times. You wrote it like you lived it." She burst out laughing. "Or died it!"

I felt an unexpected wave of sorrow. But why? I asked myself. It was my decision to publish the book, even over my brother Jimmy's strong protests. He feared that one day our parents would find the story, read it, and see how similar the story was to that of the life of their dead daughter. Especially with the name Shari Cooper on the spine. But I felt the book was too important to be left in a desk drawer. Besides, I needed another best-seller. *Remember Me* had been out only a month, but already it had sold over a million copies.

My sorrow had nothing to do with publishing or the number of copies sold, however. The story was, after all, the story of my life and death. It felt weird to sit and sign *Remember Me* like any other book. But my expression was kind as I bid Kattie farewell.

"I'm glad you enjoyed it," I said.

Most of the people who appeared told me they were my number-one fans. Where do you get your ideas? Is Shari Cooper a pen name? Are any of your characters based on real people? How much money do you make? Are you going to write a sequel to *Remember Me?* Now *that* was a disturbing question, for more reasons than one. I continued to smile and speak, but deep inside my skull my blood vessels began to twist into demonic shapes and spread a thick band of pain across my forehead and around my temples. Since returning to Earth, I had experienced bad headaches off and on—as of late, more on than off. The damage was from the time Jean Rodrigues, the girl whose body I now inhabit, had taken an unintentional plunge off Lenny Mandez's balcony. I know from Jean's memories that she never had headaches until that night, over three years ago. But exactly what the damage was I didn't know, nor did I care to subject my brain to a CAT scan or MRI to find out the particulars. I suspected the news would not be good.

"Peter," I asked, "could you please get me a glass of water?"

He studied me. "Do you have a headache?"

"No," I lied. "I'm just thirsty. I'm sure they have something in back to drink. Could you check, please?"

He nodded and pivoted his wheelchair away from the table. "I'll be back in a minute."

The moment he was gone, I reached inside my purse and grabbed a prescription bottle of Tylenol-3, a potent combination of codeine and Tylenol. Without letting my fans see, I popped two pills into my mouth and swallowed, wishing I had water. I had sent Peter away largely because I didn't want him to know how much pain I was in. He worried about me, and I didn't want that. Being paralyzed from the waist down, he had so many health problems, and I hated to show any weakness. Peter returned with a full glass of water, and I drank it down in a single gulp. The drugs took twenty minutes to take effect and I bore the time patiently.

We ran out of books to sign, leaving five hundred fans empty-handed. It could happen, I knew—I was not upset with the bookstore. As I left the mall, I went down what remained of the line and scribbled my signature on pieces of paper, on kids' clothes, even. Most seemed grateful just to be close to me. The codeine was percolating between my synapses and I felt good again. At the end of the line I was surprised to find my brother, Jimmy, and my best friend, Jo.

According to Jimmy, he and Jo were not going together, but were just occasionally hanging out. According to Jo, they were having incredible sex three or four times a week. Honestly, I didn't know whom to believe, and frankly I didn't care. They were both doing well. Jimmy was still working for the phone company, and Jo had graduated from college as a drama major, which, education-wise, was more than I could say for myself. I had dropped out of college the day I sold my first book—*First to Die.* It was this story I was about to make into a movie, with me as executive producer. I had gotten Jo a role as one of the victims, or, should I say, she had earned the role. She was quite the actress.

"How did the signing go?" Jimmy asked, studying the crowd. "Or do I need to ask?"

"She was a smash," Peter said. "They ran out of books again."

I massaged my wrist. "It's a good thing they did. I was getting a cramp. And everyone kept asking me about Sam O'Connor."

"Who's Sam?" Jo asked.

"Her muse," Peter explained. "They all want to know where she gets her ideas. I think it's a fair question."

Jo tugged on Peter's ponytail. *"We* know you're her sole source of inspiration."

Peter looked up at her and grinned. "And who inspires *me?"*

7

Jo and Peter often flirted, which didn't bother me, except much of it was overtly sexual, and Jo knew Peter was physically incapable of having sex. Yet I never spoke against it. I tried never to mention sex at all around Peter. It was a sore spot for him and—what the hell, for me, too. Since entering my new body, I had not made love once—the life of the rich and famous. Jo stroked the side of Peter's face. She was petite, as short as she had been in high school, although her hair was now blond, not brown, courtesy of a professional bleach job.

"I do, of course," she said.

I cleared my throat and grabbed the back of Peter's wheelchair. "I have a movie meeting in thirty minutes. Which reminds me, Jo, aren't you supposed to be at rehearsal?"

"I thought I'd ride with you," she said.

I considered. "You could do that, but we might not be on the same timetable."

"I'll wait," Jo said.

"This is a serious rehearsal. I might have to wait for you."

Jo snorted. "The big executive producer can't hang around for her best friend?"

"I don't want either of you to be late," Peter said. "Remember, we want to see that yogi tonight. He's only in Los Angeles for a few days."

Jimmy nodded. "Shari told me about him. I want to see him, too. What time's his talk?"

"Eight o'clock," Peter said. "It's in Santa Monica, at the Unity Church."

"I don't know if we'll be done by then," I said.

Peter acted pained. "You're the boss. You can be done when you want. I really want to see him. I think this guy is genuine."

I smiled. "You haven't even met him. How can you have an opinion about him?"

Peter was thoughtful. "I don't know. There was something about his picture." Peter paused. "He reminded me of you-know-who."

Peter was referring to the Rishi. I had seen the yogi's picture, and although he had had beautiful eyes, and lovely long hair and a beard, there had been nothing in his face that struck me as cosmic.

"I'll try to make it," I said unenthusiastically.

"He's supposed to teach meditation and certain kinds of breathing," Peter said. "You remember how often the Rishi spoke about such techniques."

"This yogi looks nothing like the Rishi," I said.

"You can't judge a book by its cover," Peter said.

"Not even a Shari Cooper thriller," I agreed.

Jimmy stared at me. "Shari, can I talk to you a minute before you run off?"

Jo pretended to be insulted, although she wasn't. "Private matters? Subjects Peter and I are unworthy of hearing?"

"We'll just be a minute," Jimmy said. He led me away from the others, into a toy store. Many of my fans continued to linger in the area, waving and smiling at me when I glanced their way. My brother and I stood near a stack of Ouija boards and I was reminded of the night I died. Not many people can say that.

"What's up?" I asked.

"It's nothing serious. It's just that I don't see you much these days."

"Is that why you came to the mall today?"

"I didn't come to buy one of your competitors' books."

I shrugged. "I'm not avoiding you on purpose. It's just that I've been busy. You know *First to Die* is going to start shooting in a couple of days, and we still don't know if Universal's going to let us use their large pond for the shark scenes."

"I didn't know that. I hope it works out for you guys. But why don't you just concentrate on your writing? Let your producer do all the worrying. That's why you hired him."

My defenses went up. I hate being told what to do, especially by my big brother. "I enjoy the movie business. I want to learn as much as I can about it while I have the chance." I paused. "I want to become a director."

"And quit writing? Is that why you're here?"

By *here* he meant on Earth. "No. I'll always write. I just want to broaden my horizons. What's wrong with that?"

"Nothing," Jimmy said.

"Are you upset that I was signing *Remember Me* today?"

"No. I'm just concerned about you."

"The book is sold as Young Adult. Mom will never even hear of it."

Jimmy's face darkened. "Mom has already seen the book. Yesterday she mentioned it to me on the phone."

I was stunned. "How did that happen?"

Jimmy shrugged. "It says Shari Cooper on the spine. It's on the best-seller lists. How can you be surprised? You wanted this to happen, and you know it."

"That's not true," I lied. Well, sort of. I didn't know what I wanted. Still, I longed to visit my parents and tell them I was back and alive. Yet I knew Jimmy was right when he said they'd never accept the truth, only be tormented by it. Jimmy had opposed my using my original name on my books. He said it violated the Rishi's desire to have me serve as a role model for the Hispanic community. Maybe he was right, but I liked being called Shari. I lowered my head and added, "Maybe I should have changed more of the names in the story."

"It's done. Anyway, you're right, she'll probably never read it."

I shook my head. "If she's talking about it, she'll read it. She might come looking for me."

"You're not that easy to find. Listen, I'm serious when I say I think you're taking on too much. You don't look good, Shari."

I chuckled. "You're full of compliments today."

He studied me closer. "You took pills this afternoon."

"No. I've been signing books all day."

"You may fool Peter, but you don't fool me. You speak differently with codeine in your system. How bad is your head?"

"Seen from the outside, it seems pretty bad."

"Shari. You have to see a neurologist."

I shook my head. "If there was anything seriously wrong with me, it would have become apparent in the last three years."

"That's not true. Injuries to the head often take time to manifest. I've done reading on the subject. You may have something wrong that can easily be fixed."

"Yeah, right, easily fixed with brain surgery. No thanks. I trust in the Rishi. If he put me in this body, it must be strong enough to last me."

"Having the Rishi's blessing doesn't mean you're exempt from using common sense." Jimmy glanced around and sighed. "The others are waiting. We can talk about this later."

"There's always later," I agreed.

Jo accompanied Peter and me back to our apartment in Venice, which was close to the beach. I sat in the middle. We were in Peter's van, which had been especially outfitted to allow him to drive using only his hands. The van had cost a bundle. Not that I minded. Last year I made over three million dollars, but had promptly given half of it to the government. For me I'd bought a red Jaguar, which sent up a flag for every cop on the Coast Highway. In the last six months I got four speeding tickets and was in danger of losing my license.

The rear of the van was stuffed with track and baseball equipment. Peter coached a Special Olympics team and also did volunteer work with several handicapped baseball teams. He didn't get paid for his work, so the only money he brought in was from his business of finding rare books for people. He ran it out of our spare room. How he managed to locate the books for people, I didn't know. But he did well and had a growing list of clients. The trouble was that his commission on his finds was usually low—five or ten dollars. It was more of a hobby than a business, really, but he seemed to get a kick out of it. I just hoped my books never reached his list of hard-to-finds.

"Shari told me the pitcher on your baseball team is blind," Jo said to Peter as we cruised toward the beach. Our apartment was in a nice area of Venice and had a wonderful view of the ocean. Still, I was thinking of buying a house in Malibu, where my producer, Henry Weathers, lived, but was worried about tying myself down. For some reason I felt I would be traveling soon.

Peter nodded. "His name's Jacob and he's seventeen. He's been blind since birth."

Jo frowned. "I can understand that he can throw the ball as hard as anybody, but how can he throw strikes? In fact, how does it get anywhere near the batter?"

"He orients himself by the catcher's voice. As Jacob winds up, the catcher talks the whole time." Peter added, "The catcher's deaf."

"And the batters are all retarded," I quipped.

"Yeah," Jo said with a chuckle. "Doesn't Jacob hit the batters half the time?"

Peter shook his head. "He hasn't hit anyone in

the last six games. His strikeout percentage rivals that of big league ball players. He's a phenomenon."

"He's probably just nearsighted," I said.

"He has no eyes," Peter said softly.

Boy, did I feel stupid. I touched Peter's leg. He could not feel the gesture but at least he saw it. "I'm sorry," I said. "I'd like to see him pitch sometime."

"You can come to any of our games," Peter said, quietly reminding me that I had never showed up yet. I enjoyed playing sports, but sitting and watching them somehow made me feel like a failed cheerleader. Visions of an old high school acquaintance, Candy, came to mind. She had been deaf and virtually blind. On the "other side," during my review of my previous life, I saw how important Candy had been to me. The few times I helped her at school had brought me better karma than the four years I studied to get good grades.

"The first chance I have," I said, "I will go see Jacob."

CHAPTER

II

*W*HEN MY FIRST Young Adult novel came out and jumped on *The New York Times* best-seller list—the first YA book ever to do so—I was approached by numerous studios who wanted to buy the rights to film the book. They came to me with names of movie stars and forty-million-dollar budgets. I was wined and dined and finally settled on a large studio that swore the book would be on the screen within nine months, a year at the outside. Of course, nothing happened with *First to Die,* or the books that followed. They were optioned, I was paid a nominal fee, and then the stories sank into development hell. Such a slow-moving hell—nothing ever happened there. Hollywood's a strange place. All the clichés about it are true: executives like to make deals. They like to "do" lunch. They do not like to make movies. Movies might bomb. They might get fired. Better to just option stuff, pretend they're going to make it. I got tired of the scene.

I met my producer, Henry Weathers, by chance. I was buying popcorn at a movie theater in Westwood near UCLA. Peter and I went to two or three movies a week—at least we did before I became an executive producer. Anyway, Henry was standing behind me and he made a joke about how slow the line was, comparing it to how long it had taken to get the movie we were about to see on the screen. As it turned out a friend of Henry's had produced the movie, and even though it turned out to be a turkey, I liked Henry. We got to talking. I told him who I was and the experiences I'd had rewriting scripts for executives who needed readers to translate the labels on their afternoon bottle of mineral water. Henry was sympathetic, but otherwise didn't say a whole lot. We exchanged numbers and I thought that would be the last I saw of him. Yet a month later—after he had researched me and read all my books—he called to say he knew some people who had ten million dollars and wanted to get into the movie business. Was I interested in making *First to Die* into a picture? "When do we start?" I asked.

"Right away," he said. "We just have to sell them on the idea."

I liked that answer.

That had been three months ago. We had sold the idea to the investors, and things were moving fast. We had a director and cast, and the cameras were ready to roll. Well, almost. Our director, although highly talented, was insane. He had a pregnant wife who did astrological charts, and a gay lover who painted billboards with food coloring and a broom. Our director talked to the cameras when he thought no one was looking. Our leading man was addicted to cocaine. Our villain had just gotten out of jail for hot-wiring a car and driving it off the end of the Santa Monica pier. And we had no place to put our sharks. Yes, we had rented a pool full of sharks. We needed them to eat a few of our characters. You can rent anything in Los Angeles if you know where to look. Henry did; he was an old-time Hollywood producer. He could make a few million look like a hundred million on the screen, and, as he was fond of saying, he knew a hit the moment it collected two hundred million. Henry had had his ups and downs over the years. I was supposed to be his last great up. He thought he could build a dynasty from my work.

Before Henry and I gave our presentation to the investors, he had me prepare a scene-by-scene summary of *First to Die.* God forbid the businesspeople who wanted to give us millions should actually have to read a book. I would have read the blasted thing before spending seven bucks to *see* the movie. Maybe I'm cheap. Anyway, this summary turned out to be the outline from which I had prepared a shooting script because I had to cut large portions of the three-hundred-page novel to fit a hundred-minute film. While heading to Henry's for my meeting and Jo's rehearsal, I asked Jo to drive so I could reread my initial summary to see if there was anything I could do to improve the story at this late stage.

FIRST TO DIE
by
SHARI COOPER

The story opens on a sailboat twenty miles off the coast of Florida. A group of seven high school students has been invited by Bob, the class nerd, to enjoy a weekend of sailing around the Florida Keys. What these seven do not know is that Bob has planned this weekend for many months. He plans to take revenge on these popular kids because he has hated them for years.

In the first scene our hero, quiet and shy Daniel, and our heroine, sweet and pretty Kathy, are talking inside a cabin when a scream brings them running up onto the deck. It is head cheerleader Susie who has cried out. Bob is holding a gun to her head and is demanding to have a meeting.

"This boat is rigged to sink in a few minutes," Bob says. "There are two lifeboats on board. Both are equipped with small outboard motors. Both are tiny; they will hold only two people, three at most. If you put more people in them, they will sink. In two minutes I am going to head back to shore in one of the lifeboats. I am going alone. That will leave the seven of you to decide who is to live and who is to die. The lifeboat I'm leaving is equipped with a compass and enough gasoline to reach shore. With any luck, whoever departs in it will make it safely back. The hull of this boat is rigged to blow in two places. The seven of you can choose to stay and try to plug these holes. That way, working together, maybe all of you will survive. But the odds will not be in your favor. Because you cannot survive in these waters for even a few minutes. For the last two hours, while you've all been gossiping and eating, we have been trailing slabs of beef in the water. The blood has attracted a large school of sharks.'' Bob pauses to smile, to gesture to the surrounding fins. "The beef has only whetted their appetites."

Hearing the setup, football quarterback Todd swears at Bob and rushes him. Calmly, Bob lets go of Susie and shoots Todd in the head. Todd's blood soaks the deck as he dies. Bob shoves the body into the water. While the others look on in horror, the sharks begin to feed.

"Now you only have to decide among the six of you who is to die," Bob says.

From below deck come two sharp explosions. Water begins to pour into the sailboat. Taking his time, Bob climbs into one of the lifeboats. Smirking, he roars off toward the shore.

Now the tension escalates.

Susie wants to leave in the remaining lifeboat immediately. Because she is head cheerleader, and homecoming queen to boot, she feels she automatically deserves a place. The others do not agree with her, particularly class valedictorian Randy. It is his belief that the three guys—Carl is the third male—should go in the lifeboat. They are stronger and the girls—pleasant Mary is the final character—won't be able to stop them from taking it. Carl doesn't agree with this. He is captain of the basketball team and Susie is his girlfriend. While the water gushes in and the boat begins to wobble, Randy and Carl get in a fight. Good guy Daniel has to scream to shut them up.

"Let's at least try to plug up the holes," Daniel says. "A boat this size will take a few minutes to sink. Maybe if we work together we *can* stop the water."

They head below as a group, but they are not a cohesive group. They do not trust one another. They cannot concentrate on fixing the holes because they are concentrating solely on each other. It is only now they appreciate the cold cruelty of Bob's revenge upon them. In a sense, Bob is asking them to destroy one another.

As the water rises to the deck, the opportunity to fix the holes passes and Susie and Randy bolt for the raft. They are in it and ready to push off through the surrounding fins when Carl jumps in with them. Ironically, he accidentally knocks his girlfriend into the water. Susie's screams rend the air as the sharks tear her to pieces. Horrified, Carl blames Randy for her death, and the two get into a shoving match. In the end, of course, they both end up falling into the water and get eaten alive.

Now there are only three left: Daniel, Kathy, and Mary. They shove off in the lifeboat just as the mother sailboat goes under, but they do not head straight for shore. Something is bothering Daniel.

"Bob has planned this so carefully," he says, "that he must know if even one of us survives, he will go to jail for the rest of his life. There must be another level to his revenge. He emphasized how we have a compass, plenty of gasoline. But I'm certain if we head straight for shore we won't make it. He'll be waiting for us some-where between here and there, and he has a gun."

Daniel convinces the others that Bob must be just out of sight, watching them through binoculars to see what they're going to do. Daniel advises them to head *away* from shore. The girls immediately consent because what Daniel says makes sense. But Daniel knows the change in course will not solve their problems. When Bob sees what they're doing, he'll come after them. For that reason, once they are clear of the school of sharks, Daniel has them cut speed while he hangs out of sight over the side of the lifeboat, in the water. Even though Bob must be watching them through binoculars, it will be hard for him to tell how many of them left the boat in the raft. It is Daniel's intention to swim under *both* rafts when Bob appears and attack him from behind. It is their only hope, he says.

Daniel has analyzed the situation well. The girls are hardly a mile from the sunken sailboat when Bob roars into sight. He has the more powerful motor; he catches up to them quickly. While he toys with their minds, pointing his gun at their heads and quizzing them about how the others died, Daniel swims under the rafts. At the last second Bob guesses Daniel's plan and spins around, catching Daniel in the sights of his gun. To save her new love, and her own life, Kathy dives across the space that separates the two rafts. A struggle ensues and Kathy is shot in the shoulder. She sags over the side of Bob's lifeboat and her blood drips into the water. Daniel does manage to climb back on board but is held at bay by Bob's gun. Daniel can only watch as Bob tries to shove the wounded Kathy into the water. But Bob makes the mistake of placing his own arm too close to Kathy's dripping blood, too close to the water. A shark rises from below and grabs hold of Bob's arm. Screaming, Bob begs Daniel to save him. Daniel, however, is not in the mood and he allows the shark to drag him under.

The evil villain reaps his just reward by becoming fish food.

The others head back to shore, Kathy recovering in her boyfriend's arms.

"I like it," I said to Jo when I finished rereading the summary. "But I don't love it."

Jo waved away my comment. "You're too close to it. You've been over the story too many times. It's great."

"It seems too simple to me."

"Most successful thrillers are. That's why they work. There's motive. There's a crime. The hero catches the bad guy. Everybody is happy." Jo glanced over at me. "You're not thinking of writing out my part, are you?"

Jo was to play Susie, the pain-in-the-ass cheerleader. Jo could look as young as a high school kid. Most of the cast were about twenty-one. I sat back and frowned.

"I often think I should be making another of my books into a movie," I said. "One of the spiritual ones."

"You can do that next. After you make twenty million on this one."

After splitting up the shares with the investors and Henry and our crazy director, I still owned a third of the film. If the movie did modestly well, I *would* make twenty million, what with domestic and video and foreign rights. I had already considered what Jo was saying. Make what would sell before making what I wanted. *First to Die* was a huge best-seller. More people associated it with my name than any other book. Yet the reasoning didn't satisfy me. I wanted to work on what was important to me *now*. Actually, I wanted to make *Remember Me* into a movie. I suggested that to Jo. She almost drove off the road.

"You will never make that book into a movie," Jo said. "It's too esoteric. It has a sad ending. You die."

"I die at the beginning."

"Yeah. But you're still dead at the end. And you couldn't put in that part about how you came back. No one would believe it."

I laughed. "You believed it. You believe I'm here."

"Only because you are here," Jo said. "And because I'm crazy. Look, Shari, don't rock the boat on *First to Die*—no pun intended. Make the movie and make tons of money. Sell out—it's the American way. Then save the world. You'll have plenty of time—and cash—to do it."

"I guess you're right," I muttered.

"How are you and Peter getting along?" Jo asked.

"All right."

"Just all right? The two soulmates are not in constant ecstasy?"

"We're close. We're just not soulmates. Actually,

I don't believe there are such things. The Rishi said it was a distorted concept. It comes from searching outside yourself for completeness." I paused. "How are you and Jimmy getting along?"

Jo smiled slyly. "Jim and I are fine."

"You never hold hands in public."

"We make up for it in private."

"Are you really screwing my brother?" I asked.

Jo acted shocked. "We are getting personal, aren't we?"

"You openly brag about the great sex you two have."

"Then you have no need to ask. Just believe."

"I don't believe you," I growled.

Jo saw it was time to change the subject. "How's Carol doing?"

Carol Dazmin, Jean Rodrigues's best friend—and now my buddy as well—was not doing well. For the last two years she had fought heroin addiction. She would clean up her act, but then meet some crazy guy or girl and start shooting up again. Recently she had gotten off the junk only to end up in the hospital with hepatitis—the serious kind. Her liver was inflamed and she was the color of a spoiled lemon. The doctors thought she could live but would die for sure if she went back on drugs. Her addiction caused me a lot of pain. I had returned to Earth in Jean Rodrigues's body to try to help people, and I couldn't even help someone close to me. I told Jo what was happening and she was sympathetic.

"It's that neighborhood she lives in," Jo said. "It's crawling with drugs."

"It's not the neighborhood. It's Carol. Besides, I told her she could come live with me if she wanted. She doesn't want to. She'd rather get high." I sighed. "I have nothing genuine to offer people. Just stories."

"Your stories inspire people."

"Inspiration goes only so far."

Jo was concerned. "What's bothering you, Shari?"

My headache had returned.

"Something," I whispered thoughtfully. "I'll know it when it comes to me."

But I was wrong.

CHAPTER

III

*H*ENRY WEATHERS'S HOUSE was a castle built as a symbol of the good life. High on a hill above the sprawling town of Malibu, it commanded north and south views of the coast that stretched forever on clear days. There was a marble fountain out front, a pool in the back large enough to double as a small lake. Yet he had bought the place for a modest sum thirty years earlier from an actor who had gone from being number one at the box office to appearing as a host on game shows. Henry was good and frugal with money, a quality you want in a producer. We didn't plan to spend all ten million the investors had given us on *First to Die,* but decided to split it between two films. For that reason, how we used every penny counted.

Henry met Jo and me at the door. He was a short man with a six-course belly. Eating was one of his great pleasures in life—he loved hamburgers in particular, by the half dozen. Sixty-five years old, he softened his wrinkles with special effects make-up and dyed his hair the color of motor oil—then had the nerve to say it was his natural color. The thing that had struck me most about Henry when we first met was the twinkle in his eye, his goodness. He loved the movie business, even when it didn't always love him. He seemed to have a special affection for me. He had a daughter my age, Rico. She wanted to be in our movie, but her father said no, she was too plain for the part she wanted. Henry could be objective, when necessary, and that was another quality that I liked about him.

"Good news," he said as we went through the doorway. "We have a place to dump our sharks and tie our boat."

"Universal's going to let us use their pool?" I asked, relieved.

"Not unless we pay them a fortune." I started to freak out and he raised his hand to silence me. "It doesn't matter. I found a place out in the valley where we can dig our own pond."

"But that'll cost a fortune," I complained.

"It will cost us a quarter of a million when you include the backdrops and the support for the boat set. I know that's a lot of money but we'll have more freedom on our own set. We can shoot the hours we want."

"How long will it take to dig?"

"A day. It's just a huge hole in the ground. I have three bulldozers heading out to the spot tomorrow. We'll dye the water green-blue—it'll look like the Caribbean. And the backdrops can be painted by Andy's boyfriend or be computer-generated."

Andy was our insane director. "This is a huge change of plan," I said. "It makes me nervous."

"Welcome to the movie business," Henry said. "Shari, trust me on this."

"All right, but I want to go out to the spot tomorrow."

"I'll go with you. Now we have something else to discuss." He glanced at Jo. She took the hint.

"I'll go wait by the pool," she said quickly.

When she was gone, Henry continued. "I think I've found a replacement for Darren."

Darren was our cocaine-snorting star. Personally I couldn't stand the guy but he was talented, and I didn't want to make such an important casting change so late. I told Henry as much.

"You're going to give me a heart attack," I said. "At least with Darren we know what we've got. Let's keep him."

Henry got up on his toes, which he did when his sense of dignity had been offended. "Darren knows we're going to start shooting in two days and he's using the situation to demand three times the salary we agreed on or he says he'll walk. Also, he wants half of it in advance—this evening. I told him that's just not done and he laughed in my face. He thinks he has us over a barrel. But no one talks to me like that—I don't care how talented he is."

"Who's the new guy?" I asked wearily, knowing Darren probably wanted the money for drugs. The five million we were spending on the film didn't belong to me, but I felt like it did, and I refused to squander any of my investors' funds.

Henry brightened. "His name's Roger Teller. An agent at CAA sent him over this morning after Darren issued me his ultimatum. This kid—I can't tell you how good he is. Andy loves him as well. He says he's better than Darren. Honestly, it was as if Roger was born to play Daniel. He's in the back-yard. Do you want to hear him read?"

"Right now?"

"Yes. We have to decide in the next hour, one way or the other."

"OK, let me see him. How old is he?"

"Your age—twenty-one."

I made a face. "And he's a kid?"

Henry patted me on the shoulder. "You're all babes in the woods next to me. I'll bring him into my study. He can read for you there."

"Alone?"

"Yes. He won't bite you."

"OK."

Henry's study was piled full of screenplays rather than books. Henry had taught me a lot about the art of screenplay writing. It was easier than novel writing yet it made demands that were unique to the form. The main one was the limitation of space. Every word had to count, whereas in a novel I could go on about whatever happened to suit my fancy. Another thing about writing scripts I found maddening was that—with only dialogue to work with—I was unable to give my story a tone. *First to*

29

Die was a straight-forward thriller; however, in book form, I had managed to give it a haunted feeling, which was probably why it had become so popular. Now I had to rely on Andy to capture that same feeling. Andy, who was known to sleep with his film before he shot it—just to warm it up.

Roger Teller came into the study.

He was a babe. No question about it. Wow.

No problem. He can have the job.

I should never have been put in charge of casting.

"Are you Ms. Cooper?" he asked.

"Shari, please. Yes." I stood to shake his hand. "Come in. Have a seat."

"Thank you."

He plopped down opposite me on a wine-colored love seat. I sat cross-legged in an overstuffed chair. His face was perfection, molded in paradox. He appeared both strong and vulnerable. His eyes were large, dark; his intelligence shimmered behind them like reflections of the moon at night. He was broad shouldered but thin; his large hands reminded me of Peter's—before Peter died, the first time. When he was tall and blond. Roger didn't look like he would ever die. He had the handsomeness of eternal youth; the world would give him only good things, and take nothing away. In another age he would have been considered royalty. His expensive slacks were soft gray flannel, his dress shirt white. He wore a gold watch.

"Henry tells me you're a great actor," I said. When he didn't respond, I added, "What do you think?"

"I went to your signing this afternoon," he replied. "I watched as those teenagers told you what a great writer you were. I noticed you didn't know what to say to them."

"I didn't see you there."

He smiled faintly. "I hid in the shadows."

"Why did you come to the signing?"

"To see you. I read your books before auditioning for this part." He paused. "You're quite the writer."

"Thank you. What do you think of the Daniel part in *First to Die?*"

Roger shrugged. "He's a strong character. But I think I would play him slightly differently from how you wrote him."

A bold comment, from someone trying to get a part. "How so?"

"I would have him talk less."

"I'm curious how you'd do that. When there's a line in the script that belongs to him, what are you going to do? Remain silent?"

He shrugged. "I think more can be done with looks than words in some places. I may only be talking about four or five lines altogether."

His boldness continued to amaze me. Most actors pant in front of someone who can give them a job. And here this guy was indirectly insulting my writing by telling me he could improve upon it.

"Hmm," I muttered.

My reaction amused him. "Of course, if you give me the role, I'll only be an employee. I can only make suggestions."

"I don't have final say on whether you get the role or not."

"Yes, you do, Shari. It's your movie."

Now he was calling me a liar, but subtly. He was subtle about everything—the way he was checking out my body, my face. I don't know why I liked him, besides his good looks, although they helped. Oh yes. And those deep, dark eyes.

"You have read *Remember Me?*" I said.

"Yes."

"What did you think of it?"

He met my gaze and held it. "It reads like a true story."

"Maybe it is a true story. Maybe a ghost told it to me."

"Are you thinking of making it into a movie?"

"Yes. But we need a larger budget than five million. It will require lots of special effects."

"For the death scenes?"

"Yes, and some of the other scenes as well."

"It sounds huge." He paused. "Do you want me to read for you for this movie?"

"Yes, please. Can I get you a copy of the script?"

"If you think it's necessary. I memorized the section where Daniel explains how Bob must be waiting somewhere between the sunken sailboat and the shore to kill them."

I nodded. "That's a crucial scene. Pretend I'm Kathy."

"It might help if you sat beside me. We can pretend we're alone in the lifeboat together."

I stood. "They're not alone. Mary is with them.

Or is that one of those small changes you'd like to make? Eliminate Mary's character?"

"I would keep her. I would just kill her off."

I sat beside him. The love seat was old, cramped. Our legs touched. "How would you kill her?" I asked. "Feed her to the sharks?"

"No. Enough of them die that way. I'd have her die another way."

"Tell me?"

He shook his head. "I don't know. You're the writer. But there are a lot of ways to die—in the movies."

"Why kill her? Haven't enough people died by that point?"

"I think it's important that the hero and heroine are alone when they confront Bob at the end."

"Why?"

"It would heighten the tension."

"It won't work. You forget, Daniel is not even in the lifeboat. He is hanging on to the side. For his plan to have even a chance of working, there must be at least two of them in the lifeboat when Bob arrives. Otherwise, there is no explanation for why only one of them is in the lifeboat."

Roger seemed taken aback by my explanation, and I knew he couldn't argue with my logic. He acted impressed. "You understand structure very well."

"Thank you." I checked my watch. "I have to go to a lecture tonight. Let's do the scene now, please."

Roger suddenly sat up. And just like that, he slipped into Daniel's character. He required no transition period. He was like liquid mercury when it came to playing the silver star. He reached over and took my hand—Kathy's hand—in the lifeboat. The expression in his eyes changed from calm confidence to deadly seriousness.

"We cannot go back. If we do, he'll kill us. If we stay here, he'll kill us. All along he's intended for us to die. This whole scheme of who will be the first to die, and who will be left alive is just that—a scheme. Don't ask me why, but he hates us. Besides that he can't let any of us live and get away with what he's done."

"Then we're doomed," I said, mouthing Kathy's line from memory. His intensity was startling in its suddenness and effectiveness. I was mesmerized by his words, feeling as if I were indeed Kathy, trapped far out at sea with circling sharks and a madman in the area. Roger squeezed my hand.

"No," he said. "I have a plan. We have to head away from the coast. He'll come after us, I know he will. But we'll be ready for him. I'll hang outside the lifeboat. He won't see me. Then I'll swim under both boats and sneak up on him from behind."

I winced, or rather, Kathy did. "You'll die."

He smiled faintly. "I may die. But not today." He leaned over and—wow, the nerve—he kissed me on the lips! "Not with you here."

I sat back, stunned. "Jesus." The word was not in the script.

He laughed. "Does that mean I have the part?"

My blood was pounding. I had to assume he could make the blood in the veins of the girls in theaters do likewise. Yet his act had been presumptuous.

"I didn't give you permission to kiss me," I said firmly.

"I didn't kiss you. I kissed Kathy." He added, "It was in the script."

"Don't do it again."

He shrugged. "Not without your permission."

Discreetly wiping my mouth, I slowly nodded. "All right, I forgive you." I hesitated for a moment. "You've got the part."

Henry and I enjoyed telling Darren to take a hike. At first the guy thought we were kidding, then he flew into a rage, saying we would be hearing from his agent and lawyer. He spat in the pool and stormed out of the backyard, where the others were rehearsing. Jo applauded his exit. She had been wanting to feed him to the sharks since she'd met him.

A few minutes later I wanted to do something painful to Bob, the actor who, ironically, was playing the nerdy villain Bob. The guy was much as I had written him: arrogant, overweight, rude. Actor Bob didn't have to stretch for the role—he'd been rehearsing for the part for twenty years. His face was pockmarked with acne, his greasy red hair a warning flag for dandruff. He was big—six-two,

two hundred and fifty pounds easily. Had Henry found me a replacement for him, I would have fired him on the spot. But there were not too many Bobs in the world. To top it off, he wasn't chomping at the bit for the part. His parents were filthy rich. He had only taken up acting for the hell of it, and he could say "to hell with you" and split whenever he wished. Ironically, he was talented, more so perhaps than even he realized. His arrogance was all superficial, I believed. He struck me as being insecure inside.

We got into it beside the pool. Henry was barbecuing chicken and hamburgers to feed the hungry actors, and, as usual, Bob was stuffing his face. That didn't bother me—I can eat like a pig when I want. But he was drinking beer as well, belching loudly, and throwing the empties onto the lawn. Slobs piss me off; I don't know what it is.

"Hey," I said, pointing to the can he had just let fly onto the grass. "This isn't your house. Pick that up and put it in the garbage."

He gave me one of his dangerous looks. It would probably work well on the screen, but not on me. "Are you the new director?" he asked.

I stood up. "You don't need a director. You need a nanny. What zoo did you grow up in anyway?"

"You're great with those one-liners, aren't you?" As he got up, I noticed he was a little drunk. "I don't need your abuse."

I tried to be patient. "I just want you to learn some manners. We're going to be working together every day for the next six weeks."

"You're going to be here all the time, huh? What for? To beautify the set?"

My patience ran out. "You idiot! Don't you realize you're getting the break of a lifetime being in my movie!"

Bob laughed. "Your movie! It isn't your movie. It's the director's movie. Besides, it's going to flop. The story sucks."

That really got me. I mean, I knew *First to Die* wasn't a masterpiece. I had told Jo as much on the way over. It was all right for me to criticize my story, but it wasn't OK for a guy who might get famous off my name to criticize it. If I'd wandered back to Earth in a male body, I would have smacked him right then. Instead, I did what I thought was the next best thing. I threw the Cherry Coke in my hand in his face. Bob's face turned cherry red, and I thought he was going to belt me. But *he* did the next best thing, from his perspective.

He shoved me, his executive producer, in the pool.

Actors.

I landed with a big splash. The slap of water hurt my already sensitive head and my right leg, which had once taken a bullet fired by a friend who couldn't remember who he was. Bursting to the surface, I heard the laughter of the others and stabbed my arm in Bob's direction.

"You're fired!" I yelled. "Get the hell out of here!"

Henry ran to the side of the pool. Even in his vast experience, I'm sure, he had never fired his two lead actors in the space of thirty minutes. He stretched out an arm to fish me out. Bob remained where he was, a smug look on his face.

"Shari," Henry said. "You should be an actor, not a producer."

"Get me out of here," I grumbled.

Henry pulled me onto the deck. Even standing soaking wet, I was still burning.

"I'm serious," I said. "I want him out of here." I pointed a finger at Bob. "Now!"

Bob was unimpressed. "Am I fired, Mr. Weathers?" he asked.

Henry hesitated. "No."

"Yes!" I screamed. "He pushed me in the pool. No one pushes me into a pool."

"I pushed you in the pool once," Jo remarked.

"Shut up!" I said. "I refuse to work with a pig who doesn't know an outhouse from a barn."

"Huh?" Jo said.

"Please," Henry said. "Let's talk this out. We start shooting in two days."

"Excuse me," Roger Teller said, stepping between us. "I think Shari's right. I think your callous act deserves retribution."

Bob was annoyed. "What are you talking about? Say it in English."

"All right," Roger said calmly. He turned and slugged Bob in the face. Roger was stronger than he looked. He just about took Bob's head off. Bob didn't fall in the pool but on the beer can that had started the whole mess. He flattened that piece of aluminum bad. He sat up dizzily, blood dripping from his nose, his eyes unfocused. Roger went and stood over him. "Apologize to Shari," he said.

Bob glanced up, and his eyes quickly came back into focus. Roger's expression was still calm but also strangely cold. Bob had to wonder, I knew, what Roger would do if he refused his order.

"I apologize, Shari," Bob said.

"That's all right," I muttered. Despite my momentary desire to hit Bob, the sight of blood sickened me. My books were occasionally violent, but I couldn't stand real violence. From experience, I knew too well how far it could go. I went over and helped Bob to his feet, brushing him off. "Do you still want to be in my movie?" I asked.

He wiped the blood off his face. "Your movie, huh?" he said.

I nodded. "I am your boss."

He cast Roger a wary glance. "Only if we get to change the ending," he mumbled.

Roger held his eye. "I like the ending as it is, Bob." He stepped past him and offered me his arm. I took it without thinking. "Let me take you home, Boss," he said.

He *was* awfully cute. "All right," I said.

CHAPTER
IV

W E DIDN'T HAVE TO GO to my place. Henry's daughter, Rico, was about my size so I was able to change out of my wet clothes right at Henry's. Roger and I split after that, however, in his car. I left my Jaguar for Jo. It was only when we were on the road that I remembered the lecture I was supposed to go to with Peter and my brother. Sitting beside Roger in his luxurious black Corvette, the thought of a talk by a yogi from India sounded boring. The other reason I didn't want to go to my apartment was that Peter would be waiting for me there. How would I explain Roger?

He just hit someone for me. It turned me on.

Yeah, the violence made me sick, but I had to admit the guy did intrigue me.

Roger looked over at me and smiled. His teeth were white as ivory.

"What do you want to do?" he asked.

"Did you eat at Henry's?"

"No. Are you hungry?"

"Sort of."

"Do you like seafood?"

"Love it," I said.

We went to a place by the water in Pacific Palisades, at the end of Sunset Boulevard. The sun had recently set; the western sky was the color of candle flames. The candle on our table shone in Roger's eyes as he sat across from me and ordered a bottle of wine.

"Do you drink?" he asked.

"Seldom." I always felt the Rishi wanted me sober during my stay on Earth. "But I'll have one glass."

"Or two," he remarked. "I know this place. Let me order for you."

"OK."

We had lobster, burnt fiery red, and it was delicious. I ended up having three glasses of wine, toasting things I later couldn't remember. Then we went for a walk along the beach. The day had been warm but a chilly breeze came up as we listened to the sand crunch under our shoes. At some point Roger took my hand and I let him because it seemed so natural. I mean, it wasn't as if he tried to kiss me again. The wine had me feeling as if I were floating two feet above my body.

"Do you have a boyfriend?" he asked.

I hesitated. "I live with a dear friend." I added, "He's paralyzed."

Roger nodded. "I saw him at the signing."

"That's right, you were there." I paused. "I still don't understand why you came."

"I told you, to see you."

"Because you were auditioning for the part in the film?"

"Partly. But I've followed your career from afar."

"Really?" He seemed a little old to be reading Young Adult books. I reminded myself that as much as a quarter of my audience was adult.

"I've been reading you since *Magic Fire* came out," he said.

Magic Fire was one of my more esoteric works. It dealt with interdimensional travel. Realities constructed out of words on the paper. Demons who appeared as angels. Gods who were terribly flawed. Humans born without souls.

"What did you like about it?" I asked.

He thought for a moment. "It was not the kind of story I'd say I liked. But it stimulated me. I think that's more important than simply enjoying something. Do you know what I mean?"

"Yes." *Magic Fire* was a dark work. I hadn't enjoyed writing it, but felt compelled to do so. It was often that way with my books. "Do you think I should try to make it into a movie?"

"No. It wouldn't work."

I was curious. "Why not?"

"It's too abstract. People wouldn't understand it."

"You sound like Jo. She said that about *Remember Me.*"

"Jo is your friend—the one who plays Susie?" he asked.

42

"Yes."

"How did you meet her?"

"We went to high school together," I said.

"Interesting. I would have thought you came from opposite sides of town."

His comment was perceptive. Especially since being in Jean's body the last three years, I had begun to talk the way I used to as Shari Cooper. For example, I almost never spoke Spanish anymore, except when I was around Jean's mom, whom, regrettably, I never saw often enough.

"Tell me about yourself," I said. "Where are you from?"

"Chicago. Have you heard of it?"

I chuckled. "Yeah. It's located somewhere between New York and L.A. Is that where you learned to fight like that?"

He was silent for a long moment. "No. I learned that somewhere else."

I had hit a sensitive spot. "What brought you out here?"

"I want to be a star."

"You didn't act like that during the audition. You criticized my writing."

"I noticed you didn't like that."

"Hey, I worked my butt off on that script. If you don't like it, too bad. You say what I wrote and that's that." I added, "Henry loves the script."

"He's a decent man. I like Bob as well."

"Are you serious? The guy's an animal."

"But he's true to what he is. I think we'll get along."

"If he doesn't try to drown you first," I said.

"I can handle him. Tell me more about your friend who's crippled."

"Peter?" I felt guilty talking about Peter. I hoped he didn't wait for me before going to the lecture. "He's an incredible person. He's my personal editor. I bounce all my story ideas off him. Without his help, I wouldn't be nearly as successful."

"Do you support him?"

"Ah—sort of."

"Where did you meet him? At school?"

"Yes."

"Do you love him?"

His question caught me off guard. "Of course I love him." I let go of Roger's hand and took a deep breath. "Why do you ask?"

Roger smiled at me in that cool calm manner he had. "Just checking."

We went to a movie. An action flick with plenty of blood and special effects, and a budget probably ten times ours. The story line was dreadful, as usual, but I had fun anyway. Then, even though I was tired, Roger dragged me to a club and we danced for two hours to music so loud I couldn't hear myself talk when we finally left. My headache was back, and although I was longing for my pills I was afraid to take them because of the alcohol I'd drunk. While at the club, I'd had another couple of drinks.

It was two in the morning when Roger took me back to my apartment.

The light in my window was still on.

Peter was up. Waiting.

Roger followed my gaze as I checked out the scene.

"Are you in trouble?" he asked.

"No," I said. "I'm a big girl. I go where I want."

He ran his hands through his thick dark hair, looking very handsome in the dim light. The inside of his car smelled of leather, money. Despite having questioned him several times about his background, I still didn't know much about him. Like where he got his money. If he had a day job. Yet I found his secretive nature tantalizing. He didn't have to say a lot to communicate. Briefly I wondered if he was right, if he could play Daniel with fewer lines. Sometimes less was more. I wished I had more time to spend with him that night, and less guilt to hide. This close to Peter, I didn't feel so single.

"How paralyzed is he?" Roger asked as if reading my mind.

"He has complete use of his arms and hands. But from the waist down he has no feeling."

"Can he control his bowels?"

I swallowed. "Yes. But I think these questions are getting a bit personal. Don't you, Roger?"

He leaned closer and draped his arm on the top of my seat. "You don't want me to get personal?"

"Not about Peter. It's not appropriate."

"What about you?" he asked.

"What about me?"

"Isn't that the question of the night?"

Before I could respond, he kissed me again. Hard

on the lips. He wasn't kissing Kathy this time, and there were no sharks in the vicinity. Yet, as I sunk unresisting into his embrace, I felt as if I could drown. It was not an unpleasant sensation. Actually, it was kind of euphoric. I had known from the moment I saw him that he would be a great kisser. Almost as if I knew him from somewhere else, another time and place. Yet, for my tastes, too much of the thrill of being intimate with him came because it was forbidden. When he reached out toward my left breast, I pulled back.

"No," I said, catching his eye.

His expression was eager. "What's wrong?"

I opened the car door. "I have to go. Goodnight, Roger."

"I'll see you tomorrow, Shari Cooper," he called after me.

There was no transition for me. One minute I was in Roger's arms and the next I was in the apartment with Peter. He was sitting on the couch in his underwear in the corner of our living room beneath a tall lamp, reading a book. He glanced up as I entered and didn't seem to be upset with me.

God. What if he'd been looking out the window?

"Long meeting?" he asked sympathetically.

"Yes." I was close to tears. "Give me a second, I have to go to the bathroom."

In the washroom I splashed cold water on my face and quickly brushed my teeth to get rid of the alcohol on my breath. The person in the mirror—I hardly recognized her. I no longer understood what she wanted. My head throbbed. I could see the pulse of a large vein on my right temple. Still, I did not reach for my pills, because I had too much alcohol in my blood. I didn't want to wake up dead. Not again.

"You didn't have to wait up for me," I said as I went back into the living room. Peter needed his sleep, nine or ten hours a night. He tired easily; often he had to take naps during the day. Yet at the moment he appeared radiant and I didn't understand why.

"I wanted to wait up," he said, excited. "I wanted to tell you about this man."

I pushed his wheelchair aside and plopped down on the sofa beside him. "The yogi? You went to his lecture?"

"Yes. Shari, you've got to see this guy. He's incredible. I think it's him."

"Who?"

"The Rishi."

I smiled. "Peter, the Rishi is not on Earth now. It can't be him."

"We don't know that for sure. Besides, it doesn't specifically have to be him to be him. You know what I mean. The Rishi is a Master. This man is a Master. They're both one with God. He gives off the same feeling as the Rishi. He's . . ." Peter paused, at a loss for words. "I've never met anyone so at peace with himself and the world."

"Did he teach you to meditate?"

"No. But he's going to. I'm going to take his course. It's this weekend."

"What does it cost?"

"Two hundred dollars."

I snorted. "If he's so spiritual, why does he charge?"

"His organization is nonprofit. They have to charge some fee in order to support their movement. I think two hundred dollars is reasonable."

"Where does the money go?"

"I don't know. I didn't ask. Shari, I'm talking about something important. Why are you talking about money?"

I rubbed my head. "I'm just tired. Did Jimmy go to the lecture?"

"Yes. He's taking the course with me. He's really excited."

I closed my eyes and slumped back. "That's nice."

Peter put his hand on my arm. "What's wrong with you?"

"Nothing."

"Where did you get these clothes?"

I yawned. "Bob pushed me in the pool. They're Henry's daughter's clothes."

"Why did Bob push you in the pool?"

"Because he's a bastard." I opened my eyes and patted Peter's arm. "I'm glad you liked the yogi. I'm sorry I couldn't be there to see him."

"You can see him tomorrow night. He's going to give another lecture."

"I'm busy tomorrow."

"That doesn't matter. You have to come. He won't be in L.A. long."

"We'll see," I muttered.

Peter shook his head. "Shari, he's what we've been looking for. He's why we came back."

I chuckled. "You can't say that. You just met him. He hasn't even taught you anything yet. You don't even know if his meditation techniques will work."

Peter was thoughtful. "It's not what he says that's important. It's the love he radiates. Already, I think, he's taught me a great deal."

I stood. "Let's talk about it in the morning. I have to go to bed now or I'm going to fall on the floor. Are you coming?"

Peter nodded, and quickly lifted himself into his wheelchair. "You'll understand when you meet him. Everything will make sense."

I shook my head doubtfully. "Not much makes sense these days."

CHAPTER

V

I woke up outside my body. Standing and looking down to where Peter and I slept. The room was dark but I could see. Not for a moment did I think I was dead, although my disorientation was similar to when I woke up back home in my bed after Amanda had shoved me off the balcony. There was *stuff* in the air now, the same stuff that I had wandered through for days when I was first on the other side of the grave. It was everywhere, translucent, vaguely gaseous, and flowing around the room, around the furniture, through the walls. It blurred my vision but not too badly. I could see my body breathing, hear myself snoring softly. Peter stirred as I stepped closer to the bed. He rolled over and wrapped his arm around me as I slept. Being crippled, he didn't usually move much during the night. He was nice and warm to sleep beside.

There was a reason I was outside my body, I realized.

I was to learn something. What, I didn't know.

I sat on the bed and reached out to touch Peter, to stroke his head. But soon after I touched him, I was gone. Touching a sleeping person while traveling out of body usually drags one into the sleeping person's dreams. I fell fast but not very far.

On the *inside,* a slight Indian man was sitting cross-legged on a sheet-draped chair. There were bunches of flowers around him and a candle flickered on his right side. He sat with his eyes closed and Peter sat at his feet, his eyes also shut. With his long black hair and beard, the man looked nothing like the Rishi, but Peter was right—there was an aura of peace around him so strong it was like being wrapped in an angel's embrace. As I moved closer, the man opened his eyes and gazed at me. A soft smile touched his lips, and he bid me sit beside him, also at his feet. A red rose lay on his lap, and he picked it up and gave it to me.

"Shari," he said. "You are here."

I accepted the flower, the fragrance strong in my nose. Never before had I smelled anything in a dream and I wondered if other people did. The feeling of love emanating from the man was almost overwhelming. Something in my chest loosened, and I found myself growing emotional.

"Where is here?" I asked.

"It's a place to meet. The place is not important. What is important is that you came to see me."

"But I didn't go to see you. I didn't go to the lecture."

"Why not?"

"I'm too caught up in what I have to do. And I want so many things."

"What do you want?"

"I don't know. Recognition. Love. Sex. I'm a young woman. I feel I should have everything that other women have." I lowered my head. "I feel so ashamed."

"Why?"

I glanced at Peter. "Can he hear us?"

"This is a private meeting."

I continued to stare at Peter. "I've betrayed him. And I'm going to betray him again. I know it."

"You don't betray him. If you know something is wrong, and you do it anyway, you betray yourself." The yogi paused. "Peter is doing fine. Don't worry for him."

"Who are you? Are you the Rishi?"

"Who are you? Are you Shari Cooper? Or are you Jean Rodrigues?"

I nodded. I wasn't these people, these personalities. I was the infinite soul, but I had forgotten that. He was saying he was the same soul as the Rishi, that we were all the same. Yet the realization brought me no peace. I lowered my head again.

"I can understand these things when I'm with you here. But I know I will forget them when I return to my body."

The yogi nodded. "It is true we have met here many times lately. But each time you remember a little more. Don't worry—the time of decision comes soon."

I raised my head and took his hand. He did not seem to mind. His touch was gentle. "Will I decide wisely?" I asked.

He picked out another rose from a nearby vase and tapped me lightly on the head with the petals. Then he chuckled. "I hope so."

The comment did not reassure me. "Do I have a problem with my head? I feel sometimes like there's something inside me—" I couldn't continue.

"Are you afraid that it could kill you?"

I nodded, feeling a wet drop run down my cheek. Another first. Dream tears. "Is it true?" I asked.

He was thoughtful. "Come see me soon. We will see what can be done."

I kissed his hand. "Thank you. Please let me recognize you for who you are."

He touched his flower near my ear. "The rose is soft. The fragrance is gentle. You can only feel my presence, my being between my words. Remember, Shari, when we meet, to listen inside. Keep the voice of the other at a distance."

My head snapped up. "Who is the other?"

My question put an end to the audience. Suddenly I was flying over the city, high above it. The moon blazed, yet my ghostly form cast no shadow on the ground. The yogi's last remark had left me in doubt. I had no clear course. Yet I was lying to myself. He *had* told me what I had needed to know.

I just didn't want to listen. But if a Master couldn't help me, who could? I thought of my brother, my oldest guide, and in the blink of an eye I was with him.

He slept on his back in his bedroom, Jo wrapped in his arms. They were naked but covered with a sheet, and I had to smile as I looked down on them. Jimmy, I knew, was intensely private. Let him carry on his affair without my intruding. I felt no desire to touch him, to probe his dreams. As I turned to leave, Jo suddenly stirred and sat up.

"Hello," she whispered.

"Jo." I sat beside her. She didn't seem to feel me, but sitting still, she strained to hear—what? Me? I didn't know. Leaning over, I whispered in her ear, "I love you, old friend. I know I never tell you that but I do."

Maybe she heard me. A smile crossed her face. "Shari," she said softly.

I sat back and also smiled. "Yes."

Then, in another blink of an eye, I was sitting on the bed in my old room. To my surprise, my mother was sleeping in my bed, or trying to. Clutching a childhood doll of mine, she cried quietly. Close by, on my bedstand, I saw a copy of *Remember Me.* My hand flew to my mouth.

"Oh God," I muttered. What had I done?

Quickly I sat down beside my mother and stroked her hair. Her tears began to subside and not long after that her breathing relaxed and she fell asleep. I drew my hands far back. I did not want to probe her dreams, not after she had just finished the story of my death.

"What am I doing tonight?" I said aloud. "What am I looking for?"

I must have thought of him then, although I didn't do so on purpose. There was no movement through time and space. I was in my bedroom, then I was in Roger's bedroom. His place was opulent, more like an expensive hotel suite than personal quarters. He lay sleeping on his side, in his underwear. Cast in the rays of moonlight, his near-naked physique was exquisite. A young David cut from Michelangelo's marble. My hands were on him before I knew what I was doing. I gripped his head, his heart.

Was he dreaming of me?

Then I was inside his dreams, in the realm of make-believe where he wandered during the dark hours. The setting was vast—the third arm of a galaxy known as the Milky Way. A thousand billion stars burned cold in the endless firmament. Green and blue planets shone overhead. Meteor-scarred moons revolved nearby. And into all of this moved the spaceships, long, sleek purple ones closing in on white ships. Blue and red beams erupted from the purple ships, striking the white ones. Soundless explosions splashed the vast black canvas with light. Yet this was the light of death; for each of the white spheres was gigantic and filled with thousands of people.

The purple ships were not bent solely on destruction, however. Even as I watched, they maneuvered to corral in the white fleet, to capture its millions of occupants, ultimately to force them into submission. But for what purpose I didn't know, only that the invaders' ultimate goal was evil beyond words. Better to die, I thought, than surrender to *their* will.

The will of the others.

CHAPTER

VI

OPENING MY EYES, I stared at the black ceiling. For a moment I was surprised there were no stars embedded there. Yet I had no conscious remembrance of having dreamed. I sat up and looked out the window. The moon was a shade past full; its pitted surface, yellowed by the curve of the atmosphere, hung close to the sea. It was odd that I could see the marks of meteors on it without a telescope. Yet as I blinked and rubbed my eyes, my supernormal vision fled, and I was left with Peter's soft breathing, a normal-size moon out our window, and fragments of dreams I couldn't quite piece together. I remembered the yogi flying in a white spaceship beside me. No, I remembered my mother clutching a rose and crying as she asked me to sign a book for her. Shaking my head, I climbed out of bed and headed for the bathroom.

"It must have been the wine," I muttered.

After I peed, however, I didn't climb back into bed. My mind was alert. My headache was gone, as well as my fatigue. A subtle *power* swept over me, as often happened when I did my best writing. Not entirely sure what I was doing, I went into my office and sat down in front of my computer. The screen glowed eerie blue white as I booted my hard disk. For the first time in a long time, I found myself not working on a particular project. My efforts to get the movie going consumed all my energy. But I missed telling stories; there was nothing like it in the world. The strange thing about writing is that you never know when the magic will strike to let you tell the stories. In fact, you never know if the magic will ever come again.

I felt the magic then.

I opened a new file, thought for a moment, then began to type.

THE STARLIGHT CRYSTAL

Captain Sarteen smiled with satisfaction as her starship, the *Crystal,* materialized out of hyperspace far beyond the orbit of the tenth planet. The familiar yellow light of Sol glistened on the main screen, faint at this great distance but nonetheless welcome. Over a thousand years had elapsed since Sarteen had seen the sun of her birth. The travels of her starship had been vast, and the knowledge gained—invaluable. But now the journey was complete. Today was mankind's birthday. Today they would be welcomed into the Galactic Confederation, and no longer be bound by the laws of the physical realm. The contact with the elder races had come only recently, while Sarteen and her crew had been thousands of light-years away, searching for other intelligent races they feared they would never find. Now the doubt was past, the loneliness over. The call had gone out. All of mankind was returning home. Sarteen knew her starship was the last to reenter the solar system.

"Begin deceleration," Sarteen said from her command seat on the bridge of the starship. The vessel was vast, over a mile in diameter, and carried a crew in excess of a hundred thousand. It could jump in and out of hyperspace only at close to light speed; they would have to cancel out most of that great velocity before they reached the inner planets. In a split second, their last hyperspace jump had carried them over a hundred light-years. But now that they were in real space, the ship's great graviton engines would have to labor to keep them from flying past Earth. As she gave her order, she heard a faint hum as the engines were brought to full power.

"Deceleration initiated," First Officer Pareen said. "We should reach Earth inside ten hours."

Sarteen stood up from her chair and strode over to her first officer, noticing the excitement of her bridge crew as they stared at the sun and thought of the glorious destiny that awaited them. Sarteen could remember well her first and only brush with the collective consciousness of the Elders, as her people were now calling them. The feeling of coming home, of completeness, and of a love that transcended all their ideas of what love could be. It was impossible to think that soon it would be their natural state. Never again would they have to struggle, to be afraid. They would enjoy the limitless state of being of those other races that had gone before them and perfected themselves. Not only that, the Elders had assured them that their entry into the Confederation would greatly uplift them as well. Mankind was special, they said. Mankind held the keys to the knowledge of the universe. It was in their genes, they said. The twelve strands of their DNA. Mankind had been a glorious experiment and now the experiment was going to reach its conclusion.

Sarteen did not doubt the Elders for a moment. It would have been the same as doubting herself. When the Elders had linked with her mind, she realized that she was them, that she had come from them. And now she was going back to where she belonged.

Pareen gestured to the crew at her approach. "They're excited."

Sarteen nodded. "Aren't we all? It's not every day that the heavens open up. I still can't believe this is happening for us, after our long search."

"But the whole time we searched," Pareen said, "we knew we would find what we were looking for."

"You did, perhaps. You always had faith. But I had begun to think we were wasting our time."

"Did you?" Pareen asked. "You never said."

She smiled. "I'm the captain. I can never show weakness." She glanced at the screen. "At least I couldn't before."

Pareen shook his head. "I think your weaknesses are few. If it had not been for you, none of us would have survived to enjoy this day. How many times did your quick thinking save our mission from disaster?"

Sarteen was thoughtful. "But what was the usefulness of our mission? To find what we sought, we have come home. Don't you find that ironic?"

"No. I find it appropriate." He paused. "Something bothers you, Captain?"

She shrugged. "It's nothing. It's just that I feel somehow our journey was cut short. That we came to our goal too soon." She touched her chest as she stared at the sun. "I felt in my heart that it would be longer before we reached paradise."

Pareen chuckled. "A thousand years was not long enough for you?"

She had to smile. "I agree. It should be long enough for anybody."

The hours passed slowly, as time was wont to do when the present moment was not as enjoyable as the promised tomorrow. The sun grew in brightness, the outer planets became visible, the gas giants shimmering in the glow of a star that had given life to a race that supposedly could tap into universal truths. Over the long distance from the galactic core, where the Elders resided, had come a partial explanation for the purpose of humanity, and why they had been isolated from the Elders the last million years.

Mankind was the creation of the creator gods, who had been directed to this part of the universe by the Prime Creator Itself, that glorious being that could only partially be comprehended even by the brilliant Elders. The creator gods had been directed to build a biological creation in the physical realm that would be capable of manipulating matter and energy over the entire spectrum of frequencies. From the pure inexhaustible white light of the Prime Creator all the way down to the most inert matter. The secret to mankind's role was in its twelve chakras, or centers, which resonated with its twelve strands of DNA. Each center in each human being was able to tap into a different frequency. When they were "plugged" back into their power source, the rest of the Confederation, these centers would vibrate with incredible energy. The whole of the galaxy would shine, and stand as a beacon for the remainder of the universe. In a sense, being contacted by the Elders was the same as being contacted by their more subtle half. At least that was what they said.

"They are me," Sarteen whispered to herself in her quarters. "But they are not me. I had forgotten them. They did not forget me."

She was alone. Her room was dark, except for the glow of her viewing screen, which remained fixed on the distant sun, and the glimmer of her crystal column, which, by some strange alchemy, shone without an external power source. After linking with the Elders, she had been inspired to build a staff made up of different precious stones that she had collected from a dozen worlds. No one had told her to construct the thing and so far she had shown it to no one, not even her dear friend Pareen. The staff was roughly as tall as a human being. The first seven stones were set at equal distances along the top half of the gold rod; the remaining five were fixed in a silver wheel that crowned the pointed top. These last five were the unseen centers, Sarteen believed. The ones above and beyond the body. They were the cosmic centers that connected them directly to the Prime Creator.

REMEMBER ME 3: THE LAST STORY

Each of the jewels she had used had come to her as if by magic: one she had found in the cave of an asteroid that tumbled between the stars; another in the many-tentacled arms of a giant insect that had crawled out of a burrow in a tree as tall as a mountain; and still another had fallen from a sweet fruit she had bitten into on a planet where there was only one tiny island, the rest water. When the jewels began to glow, as she set them in place, she leaped back in surprise. And since then she had been unable to stop staring at the staff. It was almost as if looking at it were like staring into a mirror and seeing a goddess.

"How did I forget?" she asked the crystal staff.

The communicator on her desk beeped. "Yes?" she said.

"Pareen here. Something is terribly wrong."

"Specify?"

"Our fleet is under attack. A large fleet of alien vessels, with incredible speed and power, has appeared close to Malanak. The fifth planet is under heavy bombardment. What is your command?"

Sarteen stood. For some reason, the news did not surprise her.

"I will be on the bridge in a minute," she said. "For now, veer us away from Earth."

Pareen was shocked. "Turn away? But our people need our help."

"Do as I say. I am on my way."

How different the mood on the bridge was from when they had exited hyperspace. Rather than coming home to a wonderful party, they had returned to invasion.

Sarteen found it impossible to believe the Elders had anything to do with the attack, yet the coincidence was disturbing. Why today, when all sorrow was supposed to end?

"Report?" she snapped as she stepped onto the bridge.

Pareen glanced up from his monitors. "Approximately three hundred alien vessels have materialized inside the orbit of Malanak. We are fighting back, but these ships, though small, are exceedingly powerful and maneuverable. Already, in this short time, ten percent of our fleet has been destroyed. The aliens have demanded our immediate and unconditional surrender. Our admiral is considering giving in to their demand."

"Have you been able to confirm the status of Malanak?" Sarteen asked.

"It has been destroyed," Pareen said.

Sarteen was shocked. "The entire planet? That's not possible."

"The destruction is confirmed. It is rubble."

Sarteen was confused. "How were these alien ships able to exit hyperspace so close to the sun?" Ordinarily they could come out of a hyperjump only far from the powerful gravitational pull of the sun, or any star, for that matter. Gravity greatly distorted travel through hyperspace, ripping ships to pieces.

"Their technology would appear to be far in advance of our own," Pareen said. "They are able to change speeds rapidly. Certainly their weapons are far superior to anything we have."

"Has our fleet been able to ascertain the nature of their weaponry?"

"No. It appears to be a new form of energy. Our shields can stand against it for only a short time."

"Has Earth been attacked?" Sarteen asked.

"Not yet. But many of the alien vessels are moving in that direction."

"Have we any communication with the alien fleet, besides the ultimatum?"

"No, Captain."

"Have you altered our course to head away from Earth?"

"Yes. But to what purpose?" Pareen was angry. "Our place is with our people."

Sarteen ignored him for a moment. "Put the relative positions of our ship, the alien ships, and our fleet on the viewing screen."

"Captain?"

"Do it!"

Pareen manipulated the controls. A mass of purple and white lights appeared. Their own vessels outnumbered the aliens three to one, but as she watched several white dots blinked, and then vanished altogether. Surrender seemed the only course—for the others.

"We are still far from Earth," she said aloud, talking to herself. "We might be able to escape." She turned to Pareen. "Are any of the alien ships heading our way?"

Pareen consulted his instrument. "One seems to be breaking away from the main pack. It's accelerating sharply." He looked up, fear in his eyes. "It's coming in our direction."

"How long before it reaches us?" Sarteen asked.

"At its present rate of acceleration, four hours. We

would not be able to return to near light speed and make a jump through hyperspace before then."

"How much time do we need to regain enough velocity?"

"Five hours."

Sarteen was thoughtful. "The ship that's chasing us might not be able to keep up its present rate of acceleration."

"I wouldn't count on it. I think we have to surrender."

"We will not surrender!" Sarteen shouted at him.

Pareen stepped toward her. "Then turn our ship around and let's fight. Let's at least have a noble end. Why do we run?"

"Because perhaps this is the end. The end of everything. But we can't let it finish, not like this. If humanity is so special, as the Elders say, we must survive."

Pareen sneered. "You believe anything they said after this?"

Sarteen was surprised that he automatically assumed the Elders were responsible for the attack. Yet as she glanced around the bridge, she saw the rest of her crew nodding agreement.

"We do not know who is in these alien ships," she said quietly.

Pareen burned with bitterness. "Of course we do. The Elders told us to recall all our ships so that they would all be in one place, easy to wipe out. Then this murderous fleet materializes. They must have intended to exterminate us from the beginning."

"But when we linked minds with them," Sarteen said, "their love was so great."

"They cast a spell over us. And we fell for it."

"No," Sarteen said. "I trust in that love. It was real."

"So is the ship that chases us. Love will not turn back its energy beams. We either turn and fight or we surrender. There is nowhere to run."

"There is the whole universe." Sarteen considered. "If we could gain an extra hour, we would be able to jump into hyperspace. Then we would be safe."

"The mathematics of their speed versus our speed will not give us that hour," Pareen said. "It is a simple fact."

"We have to slow them down, catch them by surprise." Sarteen pointed to Pareen's monitors. "In three hours we will reenter the cometary cloud. Find me a gaseous cloud."

"This far out, comets have no tails or gas surrounding them. It is only when they approach the sun that they begin to boil and throw off material. You know that—it is elementary astronomy."

"Yes, I do know that, Pareen. What I am asking of you is to find me a gaseous cloud of even *minute* size, which you should be able to locate up ahead of us. Not all comets are simple balls of ice out here. Some have faint coronas."

"May I ask the purpose of finding such a *minute* cloud? It will not stop the alien ship that chases us, I can tell you that now."

"But it will provide the camouflage we need to deposit thousands of nanoeggs in it."

Understanding crossed Pareen's face. The nanoeggs were the invention of the *Crystal*'s scientists, a weapon they had put together during the centuries they had explored far from home. A nanoegg was only as large as

67

a chicken egg, but contained within it a million tons of compressed antimatter—sealed inside a magnetic bottle. When matter and antimatter collided, the release of energy was phenomenal, complete. One nanoegg could wipe out an entire planet. The corona of a sleeping comet could disguise the presence of their eggs, and if the alien ship were to unexpectedly sweep through them, chasing in their wake, it should explode, shields or no shields. Pareen nodded as he considered her strategy.

"We must release the eggs with the alien ship practically on top of us," he said. "Otherwise the eggs— sharing our high velocity—will sweep out of the corona."

"True. But we can fire the eggs into our wake at high speed. There will be room for error."

Pareen shook his head. "Not much. If their weapons and engines are so superior, we must assume their sensors are likewise. The eggs must make contact with the alien vessel inside the corona or else they will be spotted and avoided."

"It is worth the risk. Especially when we don't have another option." She stepped toward the elevator. "Let me know when you have located a suitable cometary cloud. I will be in my quarters."

"Why are you leaving the bridge at a time like this?"

"I have to see to something important," Sarteen said.

I stopped writing. Tiredness had begun to creep back in. Besides, I didn't know what happened next. I didn't understand half of what I had written. *Twelve* strands of DNA that reverberated with twelve chakras? I knew that humans had *two* strands of DNA, spun in a double helix shape. I did not know what a chakra was; the word had just come to me as I wrote. I didn't even know if Sarteen was right, if the Elders were behind the attack or not.

Yet I loved the story, the feel of it, the mental pictures and feelings it evoked in me. Often I started a story simply with a single powerful image and waited to see where it went. Backing up what I had written onto the hard disk, and onto a floppy, I turned off my computer and crawled back into bed beside Peter. Just as I began to doze off, another piece of my dream came back to me, or I thought it did. I had been talking to Roger and we had been discussing this very tale. The thought made me smile. I had only known Roger a few hours and already he had inspired a story.

CHAPTER

VII

*A*T THE CONSTRUCTION SITE the next day, I came close to losing my mind. I could not see how this hole in the ground—even with the bulldozers plowing hard and Andy's gay lover painting wildly—was going to look like the Caribbean anytime in the next year. I told Henry as much, in a surprisingly hysterical voice.

"It will be perfect," he said. "You're a writer, not a director. You don't understand the magic of camera angles and film splicing. Remember, the sailboat set piece is complete. We just have to tow it over here from the studio."

I stepped to the edge of the wide pit. "When we fill this with water," I said. "Won't the water just soak into the ground?"

"Some will. We'll just put in more."

"And you're going to color the water? Will the sharks like that?"

"The sharks don't have a contract. They have to like it."

I chuckled. "What if someone falls into the water?"

Henry lost his easy manner. "We don't joke about that. No one gets near the sharks while they're feeding."

"Do we have to feed them?" It was a stupid question, I knew.

"We have to *film* them feeding. It's in the script you wrote. That reminds me. We won't be shooting here tomorrow. We'll be on the waterproof set at Warner's. We're doing the below deck flood scene first."

"That's a big change. When did that happen?"

"This morning. It's movie biz. You have to be flexible. We can't get the Warner's set next week. We have to take it tomorrow and we can't have any screwups. We have only two days to shoot, unless we want to pay an additional thirty thousand and wait until next month. Anyway, that's not the problem. It's Lucille, who plays Mary."

"I know who Lucille is. What's wrong with her?"

"She can't swim."

"What?" I asked.

"You heard me."

"So? She doesn't have a swimming scene."

"Andy told her that. But she's nervous about tomorrow. The water will be up to her chest. Andy's afraid she's going to freak. They both want you to rewrite it so that Mary doesn't have to be below deck while the others are trying to plug the holes in the ship."

"That's out of the question. The whole point of the scene is that they're eying one another to see who will make a break for the remaining lifeboat. How are we going to explain their faith in Mary?"

"I don't know," Henry said. "You're the writer."

"It can't be done. Lucille will just have to set aside her fears if she wants to be in this movie."

"We can't fire her," Henry said. "We fired two people yesterday."

"One. That's another thing that annoys me. Why did you stick up for Bob?"

"I didn't 'stick up' for him. He's impossible to replace at the last minute. I was simply trying to mediate the crisis. And then, in the end, you asked him to stay."

"I was afraid Roger was going to hit him again."

Henry's face darkened. "Did you see the way he hit Bob? Like he wouldn't have minded killing him?"

I waved my hand. "Roger's all right. I think he grew up in a tough part of Chicago. He actually likes Bob. I talked to him after we left your house."

"Can he swim?"

"I don't know. We didn't go swimming." I paused. "But it's an important question. He has a big swim scene. You know, now that I think about it, we didn't ask anybody if they could swim."

Henry laughed. *"You* didn't. I was only joking a second ago. It was the first thing I asked Roger. Let's worry about this Mary/Lucille thing tomorrow. I'm sure Andy can shoot it so that Lucille doesn't feel like she's going to die." He paused. "You look tired. Preproduction jitters? Trouble sleeping?"

I rubbed my bloodshot eyes. "I was up late writing."

"A new story? What's it about?"

I had to smile. "I don't know. I have to write more. Maybe one of the characters will eventually tell me."

"I'm sure it'll sell millions."

I shrugged. "It's a different kind of story. It may not sell at all."

Just then Roger drove up in his sleek black Corvette with the top down. Dressed entirely in black, and wearing black shades, he looked like the star I hoped my movie would make him. As I walked toward his car, leaving Henry to deal with the bulldozer men, I realized I hadn't asked him about his acting background. Not that it mattered. When someone had it, they had it. And Roger definitely had it.

But what is it? *Sex? Huh, Shari?*

"Hi," I said. "How did you find this place?"

"The director told me where it was."

"Andy? Isn't he conducting rehearsals?"

"Yes."

"Aren't you supposed to be there?"

Roger laughed. "The boss is back."

I softened. "I'm sorry. I was just wondering."

"Andy told us we could take a ninety-minute

break. We've been going at it since eight this morning." Roger glanced at his watch. "I thought maybe you and I could have lunch together."

"I'd love to, but I already have plans." I was supposed to pick up Peter and have lunch with him. He was coaching the future Cy Young award winner that afternoon, the blind one. But . . . Roger had such a beautiful jawline, and his body looked as if it had been programmed into a computer—to my specifications—before being stamped out. I added, "Maybe tomorrow."

"We'll be all wet tomorrow." He looked me up and down. "Lightning only strikes once."

"Is that what you are? Lightning?"

He leaned out of his car, brushing my bare arm. "No. I'm destiny. And it only knocks once. Come with me. We'll have fun. You can call your friend and tell him you were held up."

"Oh, I wasn't having lunch with anyone," I lied, and hated myself for it. "I was just busy with Henry." I stopped and giggled nervously. "Hell, why not? Where do you want to go?"

He spoke in a sinister voice. "Somewhere dark and quiet."

I continued to giggle. "I'm not drinking any wine. I'm not falling for that trick again."

He clasped my hand. "Did you fall, Shari? Is that what happened?"

I didn't know what to say. I said nothing.

Roger had expensive tastes. We went to the restaurant inside the Beverly Hills Hotel, and after we were seated, I found out that was where he was staying.

"But this place must cost five hundred a night," I said.

"My suite is actually closer to a thousand a night. Why are you so shocked? You make twenty times that a day."

"But—" I began.

"But I'm not a famous writer like you?" Roger asked.

"I wasn't going to say that."

"But you were thinking it." He shrugged. "I come from an affluent background."

I remembered my comment to Henry about Roger's background. "What does your father do?" I asked.

"He's dead."

"What did he do?"

"I never knew my father or mother."

"Are you adopted?"

"In a manner of speaking. Tell me about your father."

I thought of Jean's father. "He died when I was young."

"Where did you grow up?"

"In east L.A."

"But Jo's from Huntington Beach. And you said the two of you went to high school together."

I hesitated. "We did. Didn't Jo tell you we did?"

"Yes. But I don't see how it's possible." He raised a hand as I began to protest. "It doesn't matter. I have my secrets. You have your secrets. There's nothing wrong with that."

I held his eye a heartbeat too long to deny that what he had just said wasn't true. "I don't have many secrets," I said softly. There was something about his eyes that was so familiar. My response amused him.

"You have a few more every day, Shari."

He was referring to my being with him last night, this afternoon. His comment should have been enough to make me get up and leave. Yet I stayed. Curiosity and pride kept me in my seat.

"We're both adults," I said. "Tell me about your adopted parents?"

"They were good people." He changed the subject. "Where did you learn to write?"

"I'm self-taught."

"But you must have some inspiration?"

I had to smile. "Are you asking me where I get my ideas?"

"Why is that funny?"

"Everyone asks me that." I paused. "There's a troll in my bedroom closet. He inspires me."

"Have you ever met him?"

"He comes out occasionally."

Roger leaned over and took my hand, studying my palm, holding it close to the candle. Close enough that I felt its heat. His face was serious.

"You know, they say you can read a person's whole life in the lines of their palm." He stroked my open hand gently with his fingertips—the sensation was delicious. He traced a line that led from beneath my small finger in a straight line below my other fingers. "This is your heart line. It predicts your love life."

"How is it?" I asked.

"It forks at the end. A fork in one of the major lines shows great power in that area of life. You have a big heart, Jean. You're compassionate and kind. But your heart line is also splintered." He pointed to a spot one-third of the way down the line. "Here, where the break is, you're about twenty-one years old."

"What does a splinter mean?"

"That your heart will be divided at that time."

"But I'm twenty-one now."

Roger nodded. "So you're in for interesting times. Let's see your intellect line. It comes from the other direction, and curves downward. You see it?"

"Yes. It's also forked."

"Yes. You're obviously intelligent. It has no breaks in it. Come what may, you will always keep your head."

I smiled nervously. "Even if my heart breaks?"

"That appears to be the case." He frowned. "This is strange."

"What?"

"Your life line. It breaks around this time in your life. In fact, there are large gaps in the line. And then, a little later, it just runs out."

"What does that mean?"

He glanced up. "It means you're going to die."

I took back my palm. "I hardly think so," I replied sharply.

He sat back and chuckled. "It's only pretend, Shari. Don't get upset."

"I'm not upset."

"You're acting upset. Anyway, the first break in your life line occurred three years ago. If there was anything to it, you would be dead already."

Three years ago. That was when I was born.

CHAPTER

VIII

*T*HAT SAME AFTERNOON I visited Private Detective John Garrett, who earlier had been Lieutenant John Garrett. Four years ago Garrett's brilliant detective work had been largely responsible for acquitting me of suicide and balcony diving. After I returned to Earth in Jean Rodrigues's body, and subsequently became rich and famous, I sent Garrett a cashiers' check for fifty thousand dollars. I made the gift anonymously. Garrett promptly quit the force and set up shop as a private eye. I had kept loose track of his career, but never gathered the courage to visit him. Until today I'd had no burning need for a private detective. Now I thought I did.

"I have my secrets. You have your secrets. There's nothing wrong with that."

Had Roger's line been innocent? Or was he trying to tell me that he knew I was a Wanderer? I would have immediately dismissed the possibility except he had gone out of his way to point out the discrepancy between Jo's story and mine. The guy was the star of my movie, I thought. I was making out with him. I had to know more about him.

The résumé on the back of his picture, or headshot, was vague. He had done some Chicago theater, taken a few acting classes. Everything he listed had been done in the past twelve months. His permanent address was a P.O. box, his home phone number—a message service. Briefly I considered trying to research his past myself, but decided I didn't have the time. Besides, I didn't know the ins and outs of detecting. Garrett it would have to be.

I could have gone to any private detective, but I chose Garrett because I wanted to see him, with human eyes. See how he was doing. Thank him again, somehow, for what he had done for me.

When I walked into his office in Century City's twin towers and saw who his secretary was, I almost fainted.

"A leg! Give me her legs! They taste so good with sausage and eggs!"

His cute dark-haired daughter, the one Peter and I had gotten off drugs—by scaring the crap out of her—sat behind the desk. She seemed healthier and more stable than I was. She glanced up as I entered.

"Hello. May I help you?"

"I cannot stop him without your help, child. If you die on drugs, he will come for you."

i took a moment to collect my wits. "Is your father here?" I asked.

The young woman appeared surprised. "How

did you know Detective Garrett and I were related?"

I hesitated. "The person who referred me to your father told me."

"Oh. Who was that?"

"I can't remember his name." I nodded to her appointment book. "I called an hour ago. I was supposed to be here at three sharp. I'm sorry I'm twenty minutes late. I got caught in traffic."

I was late because I had gone back to ask Henry what he knew about Roger. Garrett would need something to start his investigation, that is, if he took the case. The office was nice, the rent high. Garrett was obviously doing well.

"Have a seat please," the daughter said. "I'll tell my father you're here. Ms—?"

"Jean Rodrigues." I couldn't meet him as Shari Cooper. That was one name he would remember, I was sure.

She stood. "I'll be just a minute."

I was left waiting ten minutes, but finally I was ushered into Garrett's office, which had a glorious view of Beverly Hills and Westwood, gold plaques on the walls, and leather furniture. The smell of success. He was talking on the phone and gestured for me to have a seat in front of his imposing desk. Settling myself, I recalled how I had described him in my book.

He was a man on his way down in life. In his midforties, he had on a frumpy green sports coat and a wrinkled white shirt with a loosely knotted purple tie caught beneath his oversize belt. He needed a good meal. His thin brown hair was going gray, and his red wizened face had seen either too much sun or too much life. He looked burned out. He was lifting a pint of whiskey to his lips when I tapped on his window.

Garrett had found a new chef and tailor. Besides having gained weight and improved his wardrobe, I believed he must have had a facelift. He looked five years younger than when I met him the night I died. He showed no signs of being an alcoholic now. Finally he set down the phone and glanced over at me.

"I'm sorry to have kept you waiting," he said. "I have a few rather intense clients. They call at all hours and want to know that everything's going to be all right."

"I imagine that it would take an intense person to come see you."

He chuckled. "Let's just say I haven't met many normal people lately. Except perhaps you. What can I do for you?"

"I need background information on a certain young man." I handed him Roger's picture and résumé. "I work for a production company and this actor has recently been hired to star in a new film. A few members of the company feel uncomfortable about comments he's made about his past. There's a lot of money riding on this film"—I shrugged—"so you can understand why we're curious about the guy."

"What is the name of the production company?" Garrett asked, studying Roger's picture.

I paused. "Cooper Productions."

"What is your position in the company?"

Damn, I thought. He'd know I was *the* Shari Cooper before the week was out. God, what if he read *Remember Me?* I had changed his name to Garrison in the book, but that would stop him for maybe two seconds. Maybe Jimmy was right, I thought. I shouldn't have published the book, not and made it so close to actual events. I thought of my mother then and wondered if she had already read the story.

I had been naïve, however, to think Garrett wouldn't question me about why I wanted the information. Obviously he had to be careful to protect himself. I took too long to answer his question.

"I'm the president," I said. He would quickly learn the truth if I lied. He sat up in surprise.

"Forgive me for saying this, Ms. Rodrigues, but you look kind of young to be president of a company."

"Thank you," I said, hoping my wit could deflect his curiosity.

He smiled again. "What is the title of the film you're producing?"

"It's called *First to Die*. It's a thriller."

He frowned. "That sounds familiar. I think my daughter may have read that book."

"It's a popular title." I didn't want to get into a discussion about the author, so I continued hastily. "Our production company would be happy to pay you double your normal salary to research this guy.

We are about to start shooting so you can understand our need for haste."

Garrett was blunt. "Not really. What has the guy said that makes you suspicious of him?"

"He's been vague about his past."

"So? Forgive me, Ms. Rodrigues, but if he can act and stay sober throughout the shoot, why do you care about his history?"

I spoke carefully. "We have learned from past experience that it's risky to have an actor who is, say, addicted to drugs, on the set of a film." I added, "I'm sure you can understand how volatile that would make our working relationship."

My indirect reference to his daughter's past behavior had a settling effect on Garrett, but he remained wary. "What do you want to know about the guy?"

"Anything you can find out. Where he was born. Who his family is. Does he have a police record. Where he came by his money."

"He has money? How much?"

"I don't know, but he's staying at the Beverly Hills Hotel." I removed a scrap of paper from my purse. "He drives a brand-new black Corvette. I took the liberty of writing down his license plate number." I handed the paper to Garrett. "I would like you to run a DMV check on him as well. I assume that presents no problem for you."

He studied the number. "Is this a California license plate?"

"Yes."

He sighed softly. Something about the case bothered him. "My normal fee is two hundred dollars an hour."

"Then we'll pay you four hundred dollars an hour." I took out my checkbook. "Speed is essential. If you could start researching him today, it would be appreciated. Would a ten thousand dollar retainer be satisfactory?"

"More than satisfactory. Tell me, Ms. Rodrigues, are you personally involved with this guy?"

I paused as I wrote. "Why do you ask?"

"Just curious. Are you?"

"No." I finished writing the check and handed it to him. "When do you think you'll have something for me?"

"Probably tomorrow. But it would help if you could be more specific about what you want to know about him."

"I've told you what I want."

"Maybe, but I get the idea you're searching for a particular incident in his past. Am I correct?"

I paused. "I want to know if there was a point in Roger Teller's life when everything changed for him."

"For good or bad?"

I shrugged. "Either way."

I could see Garrett wanted to ask why I phrased my request the way I did. I was glad he didn't. How could I explain that I wanted to know if Roger was a Wanderer? With his charisma, he was definitely a candidate. And if he was a Wanderer, I wanted to know if he was aware of the fact. And what his mission was.

Garrett agreed to take the case.

I thanked him, left his office, and started back to Henry's to see how rehearsals were progressing. I had the yogi's lecture to attend that evening. Peter had made me swear I would come. Yet I wouldn't be going with Peter because Roger had insisted on going, too, and I planned to take him with me. Over lunch, after reading my palm, Roger had become unusually curious about this saint from India.

CHAPTER

IX

 W E ARRIVED at the lecture only minutes before it was to start. The Unity Church in Santa Monica was already full. If Peter and Jimmy hadn't saved me a seat, I would have had to stand in the back. Peter did not occupy a seat proper; his wheelchair hugged a pew near the front. Although I'd forgotten to call Peter to cancel our lunch date, I did phone to let him know I was bringing Roger. Peter hadn't minded. I could only hope Roger played it cool, and didn't try to hold my hand or anything. But *cool* was one thing Roger seemed to have no difficulty being. I wondered if he would learn of my probing into his past. Garrett had promised me that discretion was his middle name.

I introduced Roger to Peter and Jimmy, both of whom were too excited about the holy man to pay much attention to Roger. For his part, Roger was low key. He had said little on the drive over from Henry's. Peter leaned over and kissed me as I sat down. It was a brief, friendly kiss. Peter was on my left, Roger on my right. Jimmy sat next to Roger, with no Jo to hang on to—not that he would have in public anyway. Jo had wanted to come but also wanted to work on lines, she said. Her interest in the esoteric had waned as she grew older.

"Is he here yet?" I asked Peter.

"You'll know when he gets here. Everyone stands. How are rehearsals going?"

"Great. Andy and Henry think we're ready."

Peter whispered in my ear. "Is that guy your new star?" he asked.

"Yes. He's playing Daniel."

"He looks like an actor."

"Are you saying he looks handsome?" I asked.

Peter thought a moment. "Has he been in something we've seen?"

"Not that I know of. Why do you ask?"

"He looks familiar."

Interesting, I thought. I'd had the same reaction.

The yogi entered a few minutes later and, as Peter said, everyone stood up out of respect. He looked much like his picture, with his long flowing black hair and black beard. Yet his youth surprised me—he couldn't have been thirty-five. Also, he was much smaller than I'd expected, slighter. He moved with incredible grace, carrying flowers in his hands. He wore a simple white *dhoti,* a strand of beads around his neck. He entered slowly, allowing everyone a chance to greet him as he moved up the center aisle. His accent, though distinct, was not heavy. He spoke the King's English, and had obviously been educated in the language by someone from Britain. He smiled as he walked, sometimes chuckling softly. There was no doubt, he was a happy man.

Nevertheless, I found myself disappointed. He didn't exude the power of the Rishi, and I sensed his kindness but not any divine energy. I know it was ridiculous of me to want to be hit over the head, to experience instant nirvana. Perhaps I'd heard too many things about the man—my expectations were so high. As he swept by, our eyes momentarily locked and a smile broke over my own face. Yet I did not feel I was in the presence of a Master. I watched as he made his way to the sheet-draped chair at the front and sat down cross-legged. He nodded to an assistant and the lights were dimmed. Peter leaned over and spoke in my ear.

"He always starts with a few minutes of silence."

"What do we do during this few minutes?" I asked.

"Just sit with the eyes closed and relax and enjoy the good vibes."

I glanced at Roger. "We're going to meditate for a few minutes."

"I don't know how to meditate," Roger said.

"You're not the only one," I said.

As a group we closed our eyes and sat quietly. Honestly, I tried to relax and enjoy whatever was supposed to be happening, but I felt nothing, absolutely nothing, except a growing head pain. That afternoon, after seeing Garrett, I had swallowed one Tylenol-3 pill. Since this was supposed to be a holy man, I didn't want to take another and act drugged in his presence. At the same time I wondered if I would be able to make it through the night without taking something more. It seemed that lately I had a headache more often than I didn't.

The minutes passed slowly. Several times I opened my eyes to peek at the holy man, who was only twenty feet away. He sat so silently, so still, he could have been a statue. He didn't even appear to breathe. Feeling silly, I tried to see his aura, figuring it must be real bright if he was so enlightened and all. Yet the only colorful things I saw were the flowers arranged around his seat. Finally, after twenty minutes, he stirred and the lights were turned back on. As the saint opened his eyes, he smiled and played with his long beads, twirling them in front of him. He nodded to his assistant, a young man in a blue suit, who briefly introduced the yogi.

"Guruji" was traveling around the world teaching meditation and something called *kriya*. His organization was nonprofit and educational. He had centers on every continent and a large orphanage in India. That weekend—beginning the next day—Guruji would personally teach his techniques of meditation and kriya. Those who wanted to take the course could sign up after the lecture. The introduction was brief. The assistant sat down and the audience was left staring at the yogi. But for his part Guruji seemed to be reveling in an inner joke. He kept smiling, twirling his beads, and looking around.

"Now I'm going to play the role of the teacher," he said finally in a soft but clear voice. "And you're going to play the role of the students. It is like that, nothing more than a play. But it would be nice if the teacher would speak of something of interest to the students. If there are any questions on your mind, you can ask them now."

Many people's arms went up. A bombardment of questions.

"Could you speak on reincarnation?"

"Was Jesus an enlightened Master or the son of God?"

"Were you Buddha in a past life?"

"Is your form of meditation more powerful than TM?"

"Is kriya the fastest way to get enlightened?"

"If there is a God, why does he allow so much suffering?"

"Are you enlightened?"

"Are there angels?"

"How much money do you make a year?"

"Can a person gain enlightenment through sex?"

The questions went on and on. The yogi took them for half an hour, simply nodding at each one. I wondered how he could possibly keep track of them all, and how he would have time to answer half of them. Finally, however, the arms came down and he sat silently for a minute or two, smiling and staring off into space. Then he burst out laughing.

"I don't know the answers to any of these questions," he said. "What are we going to do now?"

The audience exploded with laughter; it was such a perfect response. Peter leaned over and spoke in my ear. "See what I mean?" he asked.

I nodded. "He's funny." Of course, I had wanted to hear his opinion on several of the topics. The Rishi had answered many of my questions in a straightforward manner.

"Why do you want my opinion on these things?" the yogi asked. "If I say something that agrees with your point of view, you'll be happy. You'll go home and say he is a wise man. If my opinion is the opposite of yours, you will leave here and say I'm a fool. In either case what I say doesn't affect what is. The reality is not affected by our opinions. It is what it is. For that reason I have no opinions."

An old woman stood up. "But are you enlightened?"

The yogi considered. "If I say I'm enlightened, then you will want me to prove it in some way. I will have to give a wonderful talk or else strike you with divine energy. Or I might even have to heal someone. People expect this sort of proof from someone who says he's enlightened." He paused to chuckle. "For that reason I always say, 'No, I'm not enlightened.' It's much easier that way for me."

The audience chuckled again. To my surprise, my hand went up. He nodded in my direction and I stood, feeling weak in the knees. "I would like to learn to meditate. Could you tell us a little about the technique you teach?"

His gaze lingered on me for a moment before he spoke. "Meditation is very valuable. It allows us to fathom our inner being, and gives meaning to our life. The time we spend in meditation is the most important time of all. The technique I teach is very simple, very natural, completely effortless. Correct meditation never involves effort. You see in life we do things with our body and we do things with our minds. When you want to accomplish something physical, there is always some effort. You want to climb the stairs, you have to move your legs up and down. You sweat and get out of breath. You cannot shine your car perfectly without putting a hundred percent into it. On the other hand, when it comes to mental things, if you try too hard you accomplish nothing. When it is time to sleep, if you try to nod off, you'll be up all night. You go to a movie or play and want to enjoy it because you have heard so many good things about it. But if you sit there trying to enjoy it, you get frustrated. The only way to enjoy is to let go."

"I write for a living and that is a purely mental activity," I said. "But when I write it is hard work. I have to concentrate on what I'm doing or I get nowhere."

He shook his head. "That is not so."

I forced a smile. "But it's true. It's hard work. There is effort."

"No. Thinking is an effortless process. It happens automatically. The creator designed the human brain that way. The human brain is the greatest creation of the creator. You write best when you let go, and let it flow. It is only when you settle down that you experience true inspiration. Isn't it?"

I started to disagree, but paused. It was true; I wrote best when the words flowed effortlessly. The trouble was it didn't always do that. I said as much to him and he nodded.

"That is why you will enjoy meditation. After you meditate, your writing will be inspired. What do you write? Books?"

"Yes. Scary books."

He made a scared face. "Ohhh. You must be a scary person."

I had to laugh. "It depends what time of the day it is."

He laughed with me. "Scary books are good. Contrast in life is good. If everything was the same every day, it would be no fun. You cannot have great heroes without evil villains."

I sat down. Roger raised his hand but didn't stand. The yogi nodded in his direction. "I have read that certain yogis develop amazing powers through meditation," Roger said. "They can levitate and move objects without touching them and even read people's minds. I was wondering if the meditation you teach develops these abilities?"

The yogi played with a rose. "Why do you want these things?"

"Everyone wants more personal power."

The yogi acted surprised. "Really?"

Roger spoke firmly. "Yes, which raises a concern of mine. Your followers look up to you. As you walked in, I saw many of them handing you flowers, greeting you as if you were some kind of guru. What do you have to say about that?"

The yogi was a picture of innocence. "If people want to give me flowers, I can't very well throw them back at them." He waved his hand. "It doesn't matter to me what they do. I never ask for flowers."

"You didn't answer my question."

"Which question was that?"

"Don't you think it's a mistake for people to give up their personal power? To you or any other guru?"

The yogi was serious for once. "What power do you have? You have no power. The only power is in the divine consciousness. You don't even know how to breathe, how to keep your heart pumping. If the divine stopped doing that for you, you would be dead in a moment. We do not lose strength by surrendering our life to God, to a genuine Master. We gain real strength. And then these abilities you crave—if they come, good and fine. You will know how to use them for good. But we do not meditate to gain powers. They are an obstacle to divine realization, not a boon."

"You equate God and a genuine Master," Roger persisted. "How can we know a genuine Master when we meet him?"

"You can only know him or her in your heart. There is no other way."

"I'm sure the followers of Jim Jones and David Koresh would have said the same thing," Roger said.

"Who are they?" the yogi asked.

Roger snorted softly. "Can't you *tune* into that information?"

The yogi paused. "They were cult leaders. Their followers followed them to their deaths."

"That's correct," Roger said. "I'm sure you read about them in the papers. Anyway, such people are a menace to society. They delude the weak-willed, take their money, their possessions. They take over their whole lives. How do we know you're not planning to do the same with people here tonight?"

"A genuine Master is like the sun, complete in himself. He needs nothing, asks for nothing. But for those who wish to stand and walk to the window and pull aside the curtains, he is there. He warms their path. He guides them, nothing more. He does not steal their lives from them. The opposite—he shows them how to live to their full potential."

"But shouldn't we rely upon ourselves for guidance?" Roger asked. "What do we need you for?"

The yogi was amused. "I don't know."

"Is that all you have to say?"

"It's all up to you. Just relax and enjoy."

Roger crossed his arms over his chest impatiently. He started to speak again but then thought better of it. I leaned over and whispered in his ear.

"Those were good questions," I said.

Roger shook his head. "You notice he didn't answer any of them."

"He answered them in his own way," I said uncertainly.

Someone behind us raised her arm. "Could you please tell us about the kriya you teach? What it is? How it works?"

"Kriya and meditation go together. Kriya brings spontaneous meditation. You don't have to do anything. The mind dives deep inside after Kriya. We see our emotions, our thoughts, they flow in rhythms. We are happy at certain times of the day, not so happy at other times. A person says I am a morning person. I can only do my best work before lunch. Other people say they are night people. Their lives have that rhythm.

"Likewise, our emotions and thoughts are tied to the rhythm of our breath. When we are upset, our breath is rapid. We may even pant. When we're sad, our breath is heavy. We sigh. Then again, when we're happy, our breath is long and light. We feel as if we're floating. We are breathing in the same air through the same two nostrils, but the state of our mind affects it. The breath is the most intimate aspect of our lives. The first act of life is inhalation. The last act is exhalation. All of life occurs between these two acts. Yet we seldom think of our breath. Only if we choke on something—then we quickly realize how important it is.

"Breath is the bridge between the inner and outer world. If we can handle the breath, we can handle our minds, thoughts, and emotions. Using the breath, kriya brings rhythm to our lives. You hear an orchestra tuning up. One person is playing this, another that. It is just noise. But when the conductor comes and waves his baton then everyone plays together, and it's music. Kriya brings that music to our lives. It's a simple technique."

"Why does it have to be taught?" someone else asked. "Why don't we just do it spontaneously?"

The yogi smiled. "I don't know why. It would make my job easier if it happened spontaneously. I wouldn't have to travel everywhere teaching it. The next time I speak to God, I will ask Him that question."

People laughed. Jimmy stood and raised his hand. "I would like to take your course on meditation and kriya this weekend. But I'm afraid I won't be able to do it because my mind is always wandering. Just now, when we sat in silence, my mind was all over the place. What can I do?"

"This is a common experience. Normally the mind swings back and forth between the present and the future. We feel angry about something that's happened to us, or else we regret the way things have turned out. See how much time your mind spends on yesterday, last year, when you were a child. Yet the past is the past. It is gone, finished. Why waste so much life there?

"Then there is the tendency to worry about

tomorrow. When you were in school, you were anxious about what you would do when you graduated. Then, when you started your career, you worried if you would ever reach your goals. You can spend your whole life concerned about tomorrow.

"Yet you look to the future to make you happy. I'll be happy, you say, when I'm married. Then, after you get married, you think, I'll be very happy when we have children. Of course, when you have kids you can't enjoy yourself without a house. You postpone your happiness until that perfect future date, but it never arrives.

"Be in the present moment. If you live fully now, tomorrow will take care of itself. If you are happy now, the past will not torment you." The yogi paused. "Meditation and kriya will help you have this experience. Don't worry, you will do just fine. I see it."

"Thank you," Jimmy said, sitting down.

Peter raised his hand. Our little group was asking half the questions. The rest of the audience must have thought we were desperate people, or genuine seekers. I had enjoyed the yogi's last reply. It had hit me right on the head. My mind was never in the present moment. Some of what he was saying was beginning to remind me of the Rishi. Yet he still seemed so ordinary—funny and insightful, true— but lacking supernatural powers. As he had said, I was looking for proof of his God realization. I wished he would heal someone—Peter, for example. It was ironic that Peter would ask the question he did right then.

"I am paralyzed from the waist down," he said. "Is it possible that I can be healed through meditation and kriya? What I mean is—is it my karma to be crippled?"

"What do you think? Do you have some karma?"

Peter fidgeted. "I think so. I just wish I could get rid of it."

"You want to be able to walk again? Do all the things you could before?"

"Yes. I love to play baseball." Peter glanced at me. "I love many things."

"Do you love football?" the yogi asked out of left field.

Peter stuttered. "Not as much as baseball, but I enjoy watching it."

The yogi scratched his head. "I watched a football game yesterday on TV. A few minutes of it. I kept thinking: why are all these grown men fighting over this ball? What would an intelligent race from another planet think if they were watching this game? Why doesn't someone just give them each a ball so they can relax?" The yogi laughed, as did many people in the audience. He added by way of explanation, "It was the first time I saw a football game."

Peter forced a smile. "In baseball we don't actually fight over the ball."

The yogi waved his hand. "All sports are silly. That's what makes them fun. Now, I have not forgotten your question. You sit here in what you think of as a broken physical body. You imagine you are physical, and it would take something physical to fix your spine. But I tell you that is not so. Your body is pure consciousness. The whole of creation is nothing but an ocean of pure consciousness. It is that consciousness that upholds the entire creation. You can call it God or Jesus or Krishna or Buddha—it doesn't matter. It is all the same. It is that consciousness that maintains your body in the state it's in."

"Can you tell it to fix itself?" Peter asked, a note of hope in his voice.

The yogi shrugged. "Why don't you tell it yourself? Learn kriya and meditation. Dive deep inside. There is no physical injury that cannot be healed through the power of God's grace."

"What is grace?" someone asked.

The yogi played with a carnation now. "That is the same as asking what is the meaning of life. That is a great secret. If you ask someone that and they answer you, it means they do not know the answer. No one who knows the answer ever answers that question."

"That's convenient," Roger said, a sharp edge to his voice.

The yogi laughed. "I think so, too!"

Roger stood this time. "You are vague with many of your answers. It's like you don't really know anything."

The yogi nodded. "That's a beautiful state, the

state of 'I don't know.' Meditation and kriya lead to that state. If knowledge doesn't—if you still feel that you do know—then that knowledge has not taken you to the goal. You see, first we think we are someone. We believe we are special, that we know everything. Then, as we progress on the path, we see that we are no one. We are nothing. We are like grass. It is good to live as if you are grass. Then, when you reach the goal, you realize that you are everyone. That is the flow of life. From someone, to no one, to everyone. Do you understand?"

"No," Roger said.

"It doesn't matter," the yogi said.

Peter had another question. "Could you talk about relationships?"

"I'm a monk. I'm the last person who should talk about relationships."

"Please? I really would like to hear your opinion on them."

"Relationships are mysterious. We doubt the positive qualities in others, seldom the negative. You will say to your partner: do you really love me? Are you sure you love me? You will ask this a dozen times and drive the person nuts. But you never ask: are you really mad at me? Are you sure you're angry? When someone is angry, you don't doubt it for a moment. Yet the reverse should be true. We should doubt the negative in life, and have faith in the positive." He paused and stared at Peter. "Assume that your partner loves you. No matter what happens. Remember this: love is not an emotion, it is your very existence." He momentarily closed his eyes, almost as if he were checking on Peter's injury. When he spoke next, it was in a soft voice. "It is this love that will heal you. Nothing ever heals except divine love. It is all there is."

More questions were asked: about reincarnation, the New Age, the return of Christ. The yogi danced around most of them, seemingly tired of talking. He was fascinating, not what I had expected at all. Obviously he had depth, but was also so childlike. It was hard to tell when he was being serious and when he was playing with the audience. Yet maybe it was as he had said at the start—it was all a play to him. At one point he asked for someone to sing a song.

"Singing is important in all spiritual traditions," he said. "When we sit here, with our minds busy with whatever, we are separate from one another. But when we sing together, we leave our small egos behind and merge in the group. That is a form of enlightenment. To feel as if everyone belongs to you, and you belong to them. That is something a Master will always teach. There is no hierarchy in the family of man. We are all equal, all children of the divine. The Master is the same as the student, the disciple, the devotee. The Master never places himself above them because if he did, he wouldn't be able to help them." The yogi glanced at Roger. "That's why we don't seek power. Those things separate us from each other. They lead to ignorance, to darkness."

"Does it matter what we sing?" someone asked.

"We can sing a devotional song in English," the yogi said. "Then we will chant a *mantra*. A mantra is a sound that has a specific effect. Certain mantras are for meditation. They are to be kept secret inside. Other mantras are for chanting out loud. One such mantra is *Om Namah Shivaya*. It is very powerful. We don't mediate silently with it, but we can sing it. It brings harmony to the whole life. That is the effect of its six syllables on our nervous system. Some might ask: is this a Hindu mantra? Is it Buddhist? In reality it is not connected to any religion, race, or sect. It is very ancient, before there existed such divisions on Earth. *Shiva* is not the name of a particular deity. It is that state of perfect innocence we all have inside. No matter what we may have done in life. No matter how many regrets we have, how many sins we think we've committed—that state of innocence is always there for us to embrace. This mantra takes us there straight away. Then, after we chant, we will sit silently for a few minutes, and let the sound vibrate in our consciousness, in the depths of our being. We never chant to gain something selfish. We do it only to perfect ourselves and come closer to God. It is important to have this attitude of surrender. Innocence and surrender are two keys to the spiritual path."

Before he began, however, he invited people to take a brief break and stretch. Jimmy went to get a drink of water. Peter turned to me, excited.

"This chant really gets you high." Peter looked over at Roger. "You have to try it. You'll like it."

Roger was bored. "I feel like I'm at a Hare Krishna meeting." He turned to me. "Do you want to go?"

"She isn't going," Peter said. "I want her to meet the yogi after the meeting."

"Shouldn't we ask Shari what she wants?" Roger said.

I spoke hesitantly. "I would like to try the chant."

Roger stood. "I'll wait for you outside."

Peter peered up at him. "You don't have to wait if you don't want to."

Roger looked Peter up and down, then chuckled. "You're a true believer, aren't you? You'll follow any Joe or Harry who comes along. This man is interested in your money, nothing more. When he has it, that will be the last you see of him. I pity you."

Peter was unimpressed. "I see no pockets on his dhoti. I think he's just here to help people." Peter paused and gave him a cold stare. "What are you here for?"

Roger ignored him. "Remember, we have to get up early," he said to me and stepped past us, leaving. Peter was concerned.

"*We* have to get up early," he said to me. "What is this *we?*"

I shrugged. "It's nothing. We start shooting tomorrow. We both have to be there at six."

"You're not interested in this guy, are you?"

I forced a smile. "No. Don't be ridiculous. Relax. Enjoy the chant."

Yet I had been wrong. Roger had not stood up to leave. Not yet, anyway. Staring warily at the yogi, he crept toward him. The yogi was speaking softly to his assistant; he seemed unaware of Roger's approach until Roger was only a few feet from him. Then the yogi raised his eyes and smiled.

"Yes?" he said pleasantly, so that only those of us up front could hear. His microphone was turned off. Roger stopped when he saw the yogi's bright smile, and seemed on the verge of leaving. But then he drilled the holy man one last time.

"I won't be staying for the chant," he said. "The only power in a mantra is what you tell yourself there is. It's all self-hypnosis, a bunch of nonsense. I'm not into playing head games." He turned his back on the man.

"Wait," the yogi said.

Roger glanced over his shoulder. "Huh?"

"You are a fool."

Roger was instantly livid. His face flushed with blood and he drew in a shuddering breath. "How dare you call me a fool! You charlatan! Just because I don't bow at your feet!"

The yogi chuckled softly. "You see the power of one little word? I called you a fool and your whole state of mind was transformed. Not only that, your breathing and heart rate accelerated. Your blood pressure leapt off the scale. Now when a normal word such as *fool* can have such a powerful effect on you, can you imagine how much more the sacred name of God can change you?" He shook his head. "Don't be in such a hurry to dismiss this chant. Not, at least, until you have tried it."

Roger didn't listen to the advice. Obviously embarrassed, and without saying another thing, he turned and walked briskly from the church. Peter watched him go with a smug expression.

"It looks like your star will never be a star," he said. "Not in the sky, anyway."

"Don't be so hard on him," I said, thinking Roger had been a fool to try to match wits with the yogi.

A few minutes later we sang an English song, "Amazing Grace," and then settled into the chant. The yogi started us off, then the group continued on its own, as the yogi closed his eyes and appeared to meditate. The yogi had such a delightful singing voice: I wished he would continue to chant with us. It reminded me of the melodious words of the Rishi.

The power of the mantra, said out loud, was immediately evident. First I began to relax, and the pressure in my head lessened. Then, as I let myself go into the sound of the words, not minding what I was doing or where I was, I felt the endless chatter in my mind easing. It was as if I were tapping into the peace I experienced when I had entered the light after dying. The spot between my eyebrows and another spot close to my heart began to vibrate, as if touched by a powerful magnet. A stream of gladness flowed through me at those two points. I was not imagining it; I enjoyed it immensely. My consciousness was "high up," swimming free in a place devoid of restrictions. I no longer felt as if *I* chanted the mantra. I felt it chanted itself. There was a nectar in the sound, I realized, an inexhaustible well to quench my thirst.

I felt a pang of regret when we stopped.

Only for a moment, however. Then I was just gone. I didn't fall asleep, yet the idea of Shari, of my individual personality, suddenly dropped off. I'd experienced this as well, when I entered the light after death, a taste of the soul. It was nice to know I could contact it while still in my physical body. How long I stayed in that state, I have no idea. It could have been ten minutes or two hours. The yogi's words seemed to come to me from a million light-years away. He was telling us to open our eyes slowly. Not to jump up from our seats. Drawing a nourishing breath into my body, I opened my eyes and stared at the yogi. He seemed to glow. I thought, *He must be magical.* He was twirling his beads again, smiling. Peter tugged on my arm and I glanced over.

"Did you enjoy it?" he asked.

I patted his arm. "Very much. Thank you for bringing me here."

"Do you want to meet him?"

"Yes. If he will meet me."

"He stays afterward. Anyone who wants to speak to him can."

"You want to get in line immediately," Jimmy said softly. "Everyone wants to talk to him."

I smiled at my brother. "You look stoned."

Jimmy shook his head. "This guy is better than drugs or alcohol."

Jimmy was right. The moment the yogi ended the session, the line to see him formed quickly. Fortunately, being near the front, I was able to get a good spot. I had to wait only five minutes before I was allowed to speak to him. The people behind waited at a respectful distance. The audience was essentially private. I didn't know the proper protocol for meeting such a person. Folding my hands together, I bowed as the Japanese do, figuring Japan was in the same part of the world as India. The yogi chuckled, playing with a long-stemmed red rose.

"Ah," he said in his sweet voice. "The writer of scary stories. How are you?"

I smiled shyly. "Wonderful. I really enjoyed the chant. I want to thank you for teaching it to me."

"You're welcome. What is your name?"

"Shari Cooper. I mean, it's really Jean Rodrigues. Well, I go by Shari. That's the name I feel most comfortable with." I paused. "Do you understand?"

His eyes sparkled, and for a moment I believed he really did understand that I was a Wanderer. That I had returned from the dead to write scary stories and help save the world. Yet my stories, I now saw, were nothing compared to what this man had to offer people. For the first time I sensed what I had been looking for, the Rishi's divine love. The yogi's eyes seemed to shine as if they were windows into that pure consciousness he spoke of. He was not a man like other men. Nothing in this world could shake him, I saw. And I wanted that peace for myself. Yet it frightened me that I might have to give up too much to get it. Briefly I wondered if Roger had left the church without me.

"I understand," he said softly. "Will we see you tomorrow?"

"Tomorrow? Oh, that's when you start your course. I don't know. I don't think so. I'm making a movie of one of my books, and I have to be on the set early. I know it's weird to shoot on Saturday, but that's movie biz." I paused to catch my breath. "I'd like to come tomorrow. I feel I need to meditate and do your kriya."

He frowned slightly and touched his head. "How is this?"

"How is what? My head? It's all right. I get headaches sometimes, but I suppose everyone does." I paused again, thinking that it was remarkable he should know my head often hurt. "Do you think it's all right?"

He studied me thoughtfully. Then he nodded to himself. "Kriya and meditation will help this problem. Check your schedule, see if you can come."

"I'll try." I paused, feeling silly about the question I was about to put to him. "I know this is an odd thing to ask, but are there such things as chakra centers in the body? I mean, is chakra even a word?"

He nodded. "You experienced two of them when you sat in silence."

"In my forehead and heart?"

"Yes."

"Wow. I mean, that's interesting, that they're real." How did he know my experience so intimately? He *must* be enlightened, I decided. I leaned closer, unsure what I wanted from him but knowing it was a lot. "I wanted to ask you something else. It's about myself. Who I am."

He waved away the question. "Who you are cannot be explained with words. It can only be experienced. You experienced that a few minutes ago, when you were sitting quietly."

"I understand. I've had the experience before. That's what I wanted to talk to you about. You see, I feel like I'm here on Earth for a purpose and I might be missing it. I want to do so many things, but I get so busy that I feel like I'm missing the boat, while trying so hard to catch it. Do you know what I mean?"

He nodded and tapped me lightly on the head with his rose. "You must get to know the captain better. The boat will wait for you." He glanced past me. "Where is the other?"

"Who? The guy who was sitting beside me?"

"Yes."

"He's waiting for me outside." The thought of Roger distracted me. He had left in a huff. "I'd better go."

The yogi smiled and handed me the rose. "Listen to your heart, Shari. Not to the world. The world is a place to visit, to enjoy. It is not your permanent residence. When you don't know what to do, you return to your true home."

His words touched me deeply; the way he said my name. With so much love. I felt tears well up in my eyes. "I know that. Thank you so much."

Peter and Jimmy wanted to speak to me as I returned to the pew, but I was too overwhelmed. Collecting my purse, I kissed Peter quickly on the head and said I would be home soon, I just had to drop Roger off. Outside, I found Roger sitting on a bench and smoking a cigarette. His mood was upbeat—he said he hadn't minded the wait at all. On the drive back to Henry's, where Roger had left his car, we listened to the radio and chatted about the scene we were shooting the next day. The yogi didn't come up.

Roger gave me a kiss just before he climbed out of my car. A brief kiss, it was true, but a hungry one. Enough to stimulate my appetite. Had I not still been floating in the grace of the yogi, I might have fallen right then. But that is the thing about temptation. It will always be there tomorrow, always waiting. Temptation is like the waves of the ocean gently but persistently wearing away the shoreline. Like temptation, it knows the day will eventually come when everything softens, then crumbles.

Roger laughed softly as he stepped toward his black Corvette.

He had me and he knew it.

I would not be taking the yogi's course tomorrow and I knew it.

CHAPTER

X

*O*NCE MORE, in the middle of the night, after waking from a strange dream, I went to sit at my computer. Off to my right, in the bedroom, Peter slept peacefully. Thirty feet to my left, in the living room, Peter's blind baseball prodigy, Jacob, slept on the sofa. Not only was Jacob missing his eyes— his *real* eyes, he had glass ones—he had no home now either. Peter said he would only be staying with us for a few days; I didn't mind. He had been at the apartment when I returned from dropping Roger off. A tall, gangly, black seventeen-year-old, Jacob had struck me as a polite young man. But, boy, could he eat. Before going to bed he had cleaned out the leftover turkey in our icebox and a large bag of potato chips, plus three cans of Coke. Not to mention the chocolate cake he'd eaten. Tomorrow I planned to send him to the supermarket with Peter and a hundred dollar bill to let him buy what he wanted.

I couldn't sleep because I felt compelled to write. I didn't know what I'd say. Only that it would come.

THE STARLIGHT CRYSTAL

Sarteen sat in her quarters and stared at the column of jewels she had built to represent the twelve chakras that each human being supposedly possessed. The precious stones glowed, shedding a soft pastel luster across the dim room. It was as if each stone resonated with a portion of her inner being. Even in her desperate situation, she felt unexpected peace as she sat with the golden rod and knew with a certainty that transcended logic that the Elders had not lied to them. That they had come to humanity in love and light, and that this invasion had been unforeseen. Something thrust upon humanity from a place so alien, so hideous, that it didn't belong in the same dimension. Many insights intuitively came to Sarteen in that moment. The beings that commanded the ship that chased them were evil. They wanted to dominate humanity for perverse reasons. The Elders, and the column of jewels, emanated love. Love was what gave all beneficent creatures sustenance. The beings who pursued their vessel came in hate. They wanted to create a hate-filled planet, from which they would drink like psychic vampires. They would not destroy the Earth; not right away, at least. Not until there was nothing left to suck from it. They had to be stopped.

Yet they would not be stopped. Sarteen understood that with heartrending certainty as she meditated on the column. She must have grasped it the instant Pareen told her of the attack. It was why she had ordered her ship away from Earth. The enemy was too powerful. They could not be beaten back by physical means. Help would have to come from outside.

"Or inside," Sarteen whispered to herself. Perhaps, in the eternal scheme of things, there was a reason the enemy should come at this crucial time, when all of humanity was supposed to turn to the light. Perhaps their eyes were still drowsy with sleep, and they weren't quite ready for the transition to a higher state of consciousness. Perhaps it was not destined that they should all see the dawn. But one thing was sure—she thought the enemy would erect a quarantine around Earth. No cosmic rays would reach the planet for the foreseeable future, not unless the Elders managed to break the blockade. Yet Sarteen knew that was not their role. Humanity had to be saved by humanity. She had to get her ship out of the solar system, to safety, so that in another time, from another world, the descendants of those on board could return to Earth and guide it back home to the Elders.

Eons in the future. When the enemy least expected them.

Today, however, she had an unexpected surprise for the enemy. Pareen had located a gaseous cloud that hung between two icy comet relics like snowflakes sprayed against a black canvas. As soon as they reached the cloud, the alien ship would *almost* reach them. Sarteen had ordered Pareen to adjust their speed so that these two events coincided. Once inside the cloud, they would release a thousand nanoeggs, those tiny containers of condensed antimatter that could create such a tremendous explosion when they collided with ordinary matter. The eggs would rake the alien vessel. It should explode and leave the *Crystal* free to escape into hyperspace. The other alien ships would not be able to chase them. No instrument, no matter how elaborate, could track another vessel through hyperspace.

The communicator of Sarteen's desk beeped.

"Yes?" she said.

"It's almost time," Pareen said.

Sarteen stood. "I'm on my way."

On the viewing screen on the bridge, the images were divided. One showed the two giant balls of ice that lay before them, the elongated gas that floated between the dead comets. This far out from the sun, there was scarcely any light. The cold rocks were black as coal, the gas colorless as frosty breath in an underground cave.

The other side of the screen showed the alien vessel, long and sleek, with aerodynamic fins shaped like purple talons. The ship, though clearly spaceworthy, was also built to enter the atmosphere of worlds. Sarteen wondered if dozens of them had already dropped into the skies of Earth. The last word they had heard from their fleet was that they were surrendering. Since then there had been only eerie silence. The ruins of Malanak tumbled around the sun like a belt of meteors. Sarteen took her command seat on the bridge.

"How long till we enter the cloud?" she asked.

"Two minutes, ten seconds," Pareen said.

"Is the alien vessel precisely behind us?"

"Yes. And closing quickly." He paused. "They are within disrupter range."

"If we fire, they will just raise their shields. Then our nanoeggs will be ineffective." Pareen began to protest, but Sarteen cut him off. "We know from the experience of our battered fleet that our disrupters have little effect when their shields are up."

"They could fire on us any second," Pareen warned.

"Raise our own shields." Sarteen was thoughtful. "Hail them."

"It won't help the situation."

"I'll be the judge of that. Do as I say."

Pareen opened communications with the alien vessel. Sarteen assumed they could translate Earth language. They must have been observing the Earth a long time before launching such an extensive attack. It was her intention to stall for time, nothing more.

"This is Captain Sarteen of the Earth vessel *Crystal,*" she said. "We have noted your pursuit and are curious as to the nature of your mission. Please respond."

A minute passed in silence. Then there came a voice, heavy and deep, obviously straining with inhuman vocal cords to mimic Earth language. There was much hissing in the words, labored breathing. The creature who spoke sounded large and far from civil. They received only audio, no video.

"This is Captain Eworl of the Orion vessel *Adharma.* Surrender immediately and prepare for boarding, or be destroyed."

"Why do you attack us?" Sarteen asked.

"They are charging their energy beams," Pareen shouted, bent over his instruments.

"You are now subjects of the Orion Empire," Eworl responded. "We will brook no form of disobedience, no arguments. Surrender now or die."

"What are the terms of surrender?" Sarteen asked.

"Surrender must be immediate and unconditional," Eworl said.

"Surely you can give us a few minutes to prepare ourselves to comply with your demands?"

In response, a bright blue beam darted from the top of the Orion ship. The *Crystal* shook as if it had rammed one of the comets. The lights on the bridge momentarily failed. Deep in the bowels of the ship, Sarteen heard loud screeching sounds, painful wails. The emergency lights came on sober red.

"Shields?" she called out.

"They've failed!" Pareen shouted back.

"From just one shot? What are they using?"

"Their source of energy is unknown. But one thing is certain: we cannot take another hit. Do you wish us to return fire?"

"No. How long to the cloud?"

"Sixty seconds. But we'll never make it. Release the eggs now."

"No. Are they still running with shields down?"

"Yes. They have no respect for our weapons."

"We will not release the eggs until we enter the cloud. Hail the Orion ship again." The channel was reopened. "Captain Eworl, we are anxious to comply with your request. How can we best surrender?"

"Veer away from the gaseous cloud that lies directly in your course," Eworl said.

"Unfortunately, your attack has disrupted our navigational instruments. But if you can give us one minute, we should have them repaired."

The alien paused before answering. "In one minute you will be in the cloud. That is not acceptable to us."

"Their energy beams are being recharged," Pareen warned.

"Our instruments are coming back on line now," Sarteen said hastily. "We are implementing a turn." She signaled to Pareen to close the hailing frequency and spoke to him, "Fire all our retro rockets simultaneously."

"They'll cancel each other out," Pareen said. "We will still enter the cloud."

"Yes. But it will look like we're trying."

Pareen nodded. "Firing retros. Twenty-eight seconds to cloud-contact."

"Are they still preparing to fire?" Sarteen asked, hearing the roar of the retros firing.

"Yes."

"With our shields down, can we withstand the run through the cloud?"

"It's questionable," Pareen said.

"Reopen hailing frequencies." Her order was obeyed. "Captain Eworl, in an effort to comply with your instructions, we are going to use an auxiliary power source. Please stand by. Captain Sarteen out."

"What auxiliary power source is that?" Pareen asked.

Sarteen shrugged. "I will say anything at this point." She gripped the arms of her chair. "Give me a countdown on entry into the cloud."

"Ten—nine—eight—seven—"

"Prepare to release the eggs," Sarteen said.

"Six—five— They are locking their energy beams on us! We don't have time to—"

"Wait the four seconds!" Sarteen screamed back.

The seconds passed. They would have done so even if they had been destroyed. Yet the alien beams did not strike. Sarteen was still alive and breathing when the first wisps of the cloud rocked the *Crystal.* Her eyes locked with Pareen's and she nodded.

"Releasing the nanoeggs," he said, pushing a button.

For a moment nothing changed. The eggs were too small to be seen over a distance of any kind. That was the beauty of them. They were virtually undetectable, especially inside the cloud. Their main viewing screen was now turned solely toward the Orion ship.

Without warning the Orion ship turned a brilliant white. Everyone on the bridge yelled in delight.

"Did they explode?" Sarteen shouted out, not waiting for the glare of the bombs to subside. Pareen stood hunched over his instrument panels.

"Their ship hit several of the eggs" he said. "It did not explode, but the Orion vessel appears damaged. They have ceased accelerating."

The hull of the *Crystal* protested as they plunged deeper into the cloud. The lights flickered once more and the bridge rocked. "How are we doing?" Sarteen asked.

"Not as bad as it sounds," Pareen answered. "We'll be past it in ten seconds."

His prediction proved accurate. The pressure on the hull stopped as the glare from the bombs subsided. Finally they were able to see the Orion ship. It had been seriously damaged; an entire fin had blown off and the region from which the aliens fired their mysterious energy beams was a mass of charred wreckage. As Pareen had announced, their engines had cut off. As the minutes passed it became obvious they were falling back. Sarteen breathed a sigh of relief. But they were not safe yet.

"How long until we have enough velocity for a hyperjump?" she asked.

"At our current rate of acceleration," Pareen said, "two hours, one minute."

"Does the alien vessel have shields up?"

"No."

"What if we divert all power to our disrupters?" Sarteen asked.

"With our damage, we would be forced to cease accelerating for over an hour. I don't recommend it."

Sarteen pondered, swinging back and forth between her choices. She was tempted to finish off the Orion ship while they had the chance. Yet she was also concerned about putting as much distance between them as possible. It was not necessary to destroy the enemy. The *Crystal* only needed to escape. Logic said as much. Plus she could divert all their power to their weapons and still not destroy the Orion vessel. Standing, she paced back and forth in front of her seat, Pareen watching her.

"If we turn off our engines," he said, "we'll drift with them, at least until we build up enough power to restart our engines."

"Can we fire *one* shot of our disrupters and keep the engines going?"

"No."

"Do we have definite life signs coming from their ship?"

Pareen checked his instruments. "Yes. Many of them are still alive."

Sarteen stared at the screen. "I do not trust their captain."

"For all we know, he's dead," Pareen said.

She shook her head. "He's alive. We have hurt him, but he's eager to fight again."

"You don't know that."

"I do." She closed her eyes. "I feel him watching us."

"We need only two hours at our current rate of acceleration," Pareen counseled. "Then we will be free of the solar system."

Sarteen took a deep breath. What she did now would determine whether a portion of humanity survived as a free people or not. Her head said to escape; her heart wanted to fight. She didn't know which was wiser. Feeling the eyes of the crew on her, she slowly opened her own.

"Continue to accelerate," she said softly. "Let us pray that I am wrong, and that he is dead."

Once again I stopped writing because I wasn't sure what would happen next. Plus I was tired. Six in the morning would come too soon. Glancing at the clock, I saw that I had only another hour to sleep before the alarm went off. Why was I writing like this in the middle of the night? It was insane, with everything else I had to do. Yet I didn't begrudge the lost sleep. The story intrigued me. The more time I spent with Sarteen, the more I *knew* her and respected the tremendous burden that had been placed on her. Her last decision, however, had been a mistake. After licking his wounds, the alien captain would come after her again. And he wasn't a nice guy.

After backing up what I had written on the hard disk onto a floppy disk, I turned off the computer and stumbled in the direction of my bedroom. Out of the corner of my eye, I noticed Jacob sitting up on the couch.

"Jacob," I said softly. "It's just me. Do you need to use the bathroom? I can help you to it."

"No, thank you," he said in a sleepy voice. "I don't need to go. I just heard some noise and got nervous."

I went over and sat beside him on the couch. He wore a white T-shirt and dark sweat pants. A shaft of moonlight peeped through the curtains; his glass eyes glistened in the pale glow like large hailstones.

"I'm sorry I woke you," I said. "I was writing."

"Is it daytime?" he asked.

His question saddened me. It could be pitch black and he couldn't tell. Of course, blackness was all he knew. I reached out and took his hand.

"No," I said. "It's an hour or two before dawn. You should go back to sleep."

"Do you like to write so late?" he asked.

"Not this late. This is unusual. But this story—it won't let me sleep."

"What's it about?"

I chuckled. "I don't know. It takes place in the future. Humanity is out exploring the stars when it's suddenly attacked by an alien race. I don't know how it's going to turn out."

"I'd like to read it when you're done."

"Peter can read it to you. Or maybe it will be translated into Braille. Do you read many books?"

"I listen to books on tape. I've listened to some of yours."

"Did you like them?"

Jacob flashed a smile. "Yeah. They were creepy. They gave me nightmares." He paused. "Peter's going to take me to meet this yogi tomorrow. He told me all about him. I can hardly wait. Peter says that he has the power to heal people."

I squeezed Jacob's hand. "Maybe he does have the power, I don't know. But I think the healing this man gives is on the inside. If you go to him expecting to be able to see, you will be disappointed. It's important that you understand that."

Jacob shook his head. "I wasn't thinking he could fix me. I've always been blind. I don't know what's it's like to see. I don't care that much one way or the other. As long as I can play baseball. But I hope he can heal Peter. Peter used to be able to walk—he's used to walking." He added, "I know Peter wants to go walking with you."

I had to bite my lip to keep from crying. Often I

125

went walking along the beach in the evening. But because of his wheelchair and the sand and water, Peter was unable to accompany me. Why couldn't I just stay on the concrete sidewalk that ran along the beach?

"He told you that?" I whispered. Peter had never said anything to me. Hearing the pain in my voice, Jacob was instantly concerned.

"Did I say something wrong?" he asked.

"No. Everything you say is right. Tell me, Jacob, and tell me the truth. How do you pitch when you can't see whom you're pitching to? I know the catcher talks the whole time to give you direction, but I still don't see how you do it."

Jacob considered. "I don't know. When I wind up to throw the ball, I just know where to throw it." He added hastily, "I've never hit anybody. I wouldn't play if I hit people."

"But how do you know?"

Jacob paused. "I never thought about it. Maybe the yogi could tell me if I asked him. Would that be a good question to ask him?"

I had to laugh. "I think it would be the perfect question to ask. He may or may not be able to work miracles, as I said, but you are a miracle, Jacob. I'm going to come see you play the first chance I get."

Jacob beamed. "I'd like that."

"I like you," I said. "You stay here as long as you want. I mean that."

"Thank you, Shari."

"You don't have to thank me." Standing, I kissed him on the forehead. "Now go to sleep."

I went to bed and crawled under the covers.

I felt as if I'd barely closed my eyes when the alarm went off.

God, my head was throbbing with pain.

I need a miracle.

CHAPTER
XI

*L*UCILLE DID NOT LIKE WATER. No, actually, Lucille was terrified of water. The terror could be used in later scenes because we were, after all, making a scary movie. If only Lucille could have learned to save it, bottle it somehow. But we couldn't have her character Mary screaming as soon as the incoming water went above her knees. The water was supposed to go up to their necks before they abandoned their attempt to plug the holes. Andy shouted "Cut!" so many times that I thought he would walk the first day of shooting. Finally he threw in the towel—literally, at Lucille. All the actors had to dry themselves off between cuts. Fortunately they were wearing bathing suits. We just had to blow-dry their legs, bikinis and trunks. Jo took Lucille aside to comfort her while I retreated to a corner to have a private nervous breakdown with Henry.

"Has anything like this ever happened to you before?" I complained.

"I was once filming a movie about skydiving," he began.

"Don't tell me," I interrupted. "Your star was afraid of heights?"

"No. He was suicidal. He jumped out of the plane without a parachute."

I made a face. "Did he die?"

"He didn't bounce." He paused. "What are we going to do?"

"I'm supposed to ask you that question."

Henry considered. "We could cancel the day's shoot. Call some of the others on our backup lists."

I waved my hand. "Most of them couldn't act."

"Yeah, but they could probably all swim. Mary's not a crucial role. We don't need an Academy Award-winning performance."

"All the roles are crucial. Have one bad actor in the lot and they'll all look bad. Besides, I hate to fall a whole day behind at the beginning." I stopped and glanced over at Lucille, who was sobbing into a towel. She knew we were talking about her. She would have had to be brain dead not to know. "Maybe we could give her a stiff drink."

"We could if this was a western," Henry said. "We have to face reality. Lucille can't be in this movie. If she's nervous here, she'll be hysterical when we shoot with the sharks and out on the ocean."

Roger came over. "I know what the problem is and I know what the solution is," he said boldly.

Henry and I exchanged looks. "We're all ears," Henry said.

"Shari can play Mary," he said. He raised his hand as I started to protest. "I watched you read the other day. You're a wonderful actress, completely natural, very expressive. Also, you know every scene, every line of dialogue. If you bring in someone new, we'll all have to rehearse with her for a couple of days. You'll lose time and money."

Henry was staring at me. "He has a point."

"He's forgetting one small thing," I said. "I have never acted in front of a camera in my life. Besides, I can't be in my own movie. That's the height of egotism."

"Hollywood is all about ego," Henry said. "But I agree with Roger, I think you can play the role. The camera is not as frightening as you think. It just takes pictures."

"That millions of people see," I said.

"We hope millions will see this movie," Henry reminded me.

"Shari," Roger said, taking my hand. "Your fear of the camera will vanish quickly. In this scene the camera is hardly ever focused on Mary. She's just reacting with the others. She has two lines. Think about it—we can shoot all day if you can say those two lines."

I considered. "Will I have to wear a bikini?"

"You'll look funny if you're the only one dressed like an executive producer," Henry said in his most helpful manner.

I grumbled, yet inside my heart was racing. Me, in the movies? What a thought. Besides being absolutely terrifying, it was also terribly exciting. If

I was good, I thought, maybe I'd get work in other films. Films other than my own. Anything was possible, especially for a cosmic Wanderer like myself. I burst out laughing.

"All right, I'll do it," I said.

Roger patted me on the shoulder. "Good."

"This better not be a setup to embarrass me," I told him, pinching his darling face.

Roger grinned. "I know better ways to do that."

"I bet you do," I said, catching his eye.

"Who gets to fire Lucille?" Henry asked.

I glanced at the weeping girl. "I think she's ready to quit."

An hour later we were ready to shoot again. Lucille hadn't been happy about leaving, but she was reasonable enough to see that we had no choice. Of course, we had her safely off the set before we announced I was taking her part. Bob was the only one to burst out laughing. I felt like throwing something at him.

"This is turning into a B movie," he said. "Who told you you can act? Your money?"

"Why don't you at least let me make a fool of myself before ridiculing me," I said.

Bob nodded. "But then I have your permission to ridicule you?"

Roger came up and stood at my side. "You don't have my permission," he said.

Bob gave him a dark look. "You know, I could sue you for punching me out."

Roger held his eye. "You could, but then you'd

have to suffer the consequences. And I don't mean in court."

"All right," I said, stepping between them. "This is all make-believe. We don't need hard reality here. Andy, are you ready to roll? Good. *Lights. Camera. Action.* Let's do it."

So I made my acting debut and I was damn good—in one out of nine of the takes we shot. But, hey, it only takes one great slice of celluloid— taped together with sixty other great slices—to win an Oscar. And it wasn't as if I was bad in the other eight takes. In four of them someone else caused Andy to yell, "Cut!" We each took turns screwing up, except for Roger, who was the consummate pro. Andy said he would have the camera on Roger more than on anyone else. It wasn't until later, when I saw the dailies, that I realized how much the camera loved Roger. His strong jaw line, his dark eyes—his face seemed to leap off the screen. A star is born, and it was happening before our eyes.

I didn't look bad either. I enjoyed acting. It was like being a kid and playing let's pretend. I knew how to pretend to be Mary because I had created Mary. She was me—she was a part of me. And I suppose that made me her God. Yeah, stepping in front of the camera went straight to my head. Yet, even though the experience gave me a huge rush, it didn't bring the deeper contentment that writing did. Acting was emotional for me, but constructing a story out of nothing—more spiritual.

I thought of the yogi as we watched the dailies,

and wondered how Peter and Jimmy were doing with the kriya and meditation. My headache had receded, somewhat, as the afternoon went on, but it never really left me. Once again, I wished the yogi was staying in Los Angeles a few days longer. Even though I wasn't taking his course, I planned to try to see him that evening. But Roger headed me off as I was leaving and asked what I was doing that evening. We were alone in the parking lot. The sun was still up but close to the horizon. The orange light on his face played up his strong features. When I explained where I was going, he didn't laugh as I thought he would.

"I know I must have sounded like a smart-ass at his lecture," he said. "And the way he pushed my buttons at the end did embarrass me. I admit it. I also admit that in his own way, he is a brilliant speaker. He has something special—there's no denying it."

"I think so," I said, pleased that he was being open about the subject.

"But," he said, "let me explain where I was coming from, and see if some of what I say doesn't make sense. I've had to fight for everything I've ever gotten in life. No one's ever given me a thing. In a way, I think that's good. It's made me a strong person. When I raised my concern about giving up my personal power, I meant it. I think our world is a jungle and we have to struggle for what we can get. I'm sorry if that doesn't sound as idealistic as the blissful creation the yogi talked about, but I

133

think it's reality. When I challenged him on that point and he maneuvered around it, it made me mad. I think you can understand why."

"I don't think he maneuvered around it," I said diplomatically. "I just think his point of view is different from yours. It doesn't mean that you're wrong and he's right."

Roger took a breath. "All right, let me put it another way. He's a monk. He says he's just here to help people and I believe him. That's fine as far as it goes. Maybe he isn't interested in money, I don't know. But because he is a monk, he lives in a different world from the rest of us. He doesn't have to go to work every day and scrape to make a living. Do you see what I'm saying?"

I wondered what had happened to Roger's affluent background.

"Sort of," I said.

"Let me be specific. The people around him obviously look up to him as a Master. Although he doesn't come right out and say he is one, he never denies it. As he travels around the world, he collects followers. God knows half the people at the lecture last night signed up for his course. I even saw that sitting outside. Now as time goes by, these people will idolize him more and more. They hang on to his every word already. But what happens when he gives the wrong advice? I'm not saying he's going to tell them to drink poisoned Kool-Aid or anything like that. Comparing him to Jim Jones or David Koresh was unfair on my part. But I'm saying he's a human being like you and me. He's not perfect."

"I suppose he could make a mistake," I muttered.

"Exactly. The trouble is the people around him think he's perfect. That's my main complaint. They stop looking to themselves for guidance and put their trust totally in him. I don't like that. I think it's dangerous."

"But he did say that a true Master will always teach a person to think for herself or himself. I don't think he wants to interfere with our personal lives in any way. I don't think it's his style."

"You're missing the point. He says one thing, which he may sincerely believe, I don't know—but something quite different is happening around him. Look at your friend Peter. If that yogi told him to jump off a cliff, he'd do it."

"But Peter can't jump," I said softly.

"I'm sorry. I didn't mean it that way. But Peter's known this guy—what? Three days? And already he stares at him like he's Jesus returned to Earth. That kind of adulation disturbs me. You're smart, Shari. In your books you write about how people behave, how they fool themselves. Surely you can see that Peter's fooling himself?"

I hesitated. "Much of what you say is reasonable. I think blind faith can be dangerous. I'm suspicious of cults and always have been. But I know from my own experience that the yogi made me feel better. Not just mentally or emotionally, but physically as well. I had a terrible headache when I went to see him and he took it away."

Roger flashed a nasty smile. "Well, I know how to get rid of headaches, too."

I giggled. "You do? How?"

He touched my shoulder. "A long back massage with warm oil to start."

I blushed. "I don't know. That sounds dangerous. You might do that and I might jump when you say jump."

He continued to stroke me. His dark eyes so big, so friendly. "A full body massage is especially effective at removing stress. You feel so relaxed afterward, you feel you can do anything. What do you say?"

I blinked. "To what?"

"Dinner."

I shook my head. "I don't know. I'm pretty tired. I should take it easy tonight."

"But you weren't going to take it easy. You were going to go see the yogi. Remember?"

"Yeah. I guess you're right."

He moved closer, spoke softly in my ear. "Why don't you see me instead? I won't tell Peter."

I leaned against him. "I don't know. I feel funny about it."

He stroked my hair. "Fun is good. It's good fun."

"But I did want to see the yogi. He's only here for a short time."

He lightly kissed my ear. "What will you do with the yogi? He'll say wise things and you'll nod your head and go home and feel a little more spiritual. With me you won't even have to speak. You can just lie there and feel wonderful."

I giggled again. "You make it sound tempting."

He lightly kissed my cheek. "That's what I'm here for—to tempt you."

I nodded. "I believe it."

He kissed me then, on the lips, in the middle of the parking lot, with no one around. The setting sun lit his hair on fire. He kissed me long and deep—and deep was the operative word. Because I felt as if I were falling as I sank into his arms. Down a long dark tunnel, at the end of which a white light shone, or a purple light smoldered. Which it was, a path of light or one of darkness, I didn't know. And suddenly I didn't care.

I only knew that, once again, I was going to miss seeing the yogi.

CHAPTER

XII

OVER THE PAST THREE YEARS, because I have been so busy, Peter and I have often communicated via our telephone answering machine. At dinner with Roger, drinking wine and eating steak, I excused myself to check on my messages. I knew Peter would leave me his evening schedule, and I wanted to plan my time with Roger around that schedule. To my surprise, Peter had left me a message saying he was going to a program with the yogi, and that he wouldn't be home until eleven o'clock. It was almost as if he were giving me permission to cheat on him.

And that was the question of the hour, wasn't it? Was I going to betray my dear friend? Was I going to let Roger seduce me, as he clearly intended? For all my internal dialogue concerning my situation, I had not decided where I wanted my relationship with Roger to lead. God knows I was feeling horny. I hadn't had sex since I'd been in my *last* body. True, Jean had had a few good times in *this* body, but those memories only whetted my appetite for more. A million fantasies of being alone with Roger ran through my head. What would it be like to have him give me a full-body massage? It was better not even to think about it, not while standing up. But what would it be like to sleep beside Peter after I'd had sex with another guy? Somehow, I didn't think I could bear that.

I will never find another Peter.

Yet when Roger asked me where I wanted to go as we left the restaurant, I said, My place.

It was eight-thirty.

Honestly, I thought it was safer to go to the apartment than his room. If we went to the Beverly Hills Hotel, we would just end up in bed. I thought at home I wouldn't let things get out of hand.

Yet when we got there Roger asked me if I wanted a massage.

I said yes.

It was nine o'clock.

Honestly, I didn't know he would actually take off my clothes. He just pulled up my shirt to start, and then he got some baby oil, so I had to take off my shirt because I didn't want to get oil on it. His hands felt so good, moving up and down and around and around, pressing all the sore and sensitive spots. I don't remember exactly when I took off my pants, but I do remember when he started kissing me again, and how it felt like the most delicious act imaginable in all of creation. His lips, his tongue, his hands—they were what I *needed.* If this was sin, then maybe I belonged in hell. I felt so good. Soon the oil was over both of us. The hot sweaty oil.

Suddenly I didn't know what time it was.

Until I heard someone standing behind us.

I sat up with a start.

Actually, I almost leaped out of my skin.

Jacob was standing in the doorway of my bedroom in his swimming trunks, dazed and confused, his white cane in his pitching hand. In an instant I understood what had happened. Peter had dropped Jacob back at the apartment so that the young man could relax and use the pool and sauna. Jacob had said something earlier about wanting to try them out. I had not forgotten that Jacob was staying with us, but had just never thought Peter would leave the blind boy home alone. Yet Jacob was seventeen; he was used to being out on the streets. Once Peter had shown him how to get from the pool back to the apartment, Jacob was more than capable of taking care of himself. Indeed, the possibility should have crossed my mind when I reentered the apartment. The door had been unlocked, and Peter never left without throwing the dead bolt.

In either case I had been caught with my pants down and I felt as terrible as a human being could feel and still be breathing. Before Jacob appeared, I realized how loud we had both been groaning, me in particular. Yet we hadn't had sex yet, although we were as close as two people could get. Jacob turned away.

"I'm sorry," he said. "I didn't mean to intrude. I didn't know you were home—Shari, Peter."

Hastily I put a finger to my lip, signaling Roger not to speak. Grabbing a robe from beside the bed, I threw it on and chased after Jacob. I found him sitting on the couch, trembling, on the verge of tears. Obviously, even if he had the participants confused, he knew what we had been in the middle of, so there would be no point in trying to deny it. Clearly he felt terrible for having walked in on us. Sitting beside him, I put my arm around his shoulder.

"That's all right, Jacob," I said. "You didn't disturb us. Don't be upset."

He moaned, his head down. "I'm so sorry."

I forced a laugh. "No. You have no reason to be sorry. Hey, how was the pool? Pretty cool, huh?"

He looked up, or at least, raised his head. "I liked it. I've never been in a pool before."

"Really? Did you go in the sauna?"

"Yeah. Boy, it was hot in there. I couldn't stop sweating."

I giggled nervously. "That's what you're supposed to do, silly. Hey, can I get you something to drink?"

"Sure."

"A Coke? Three Cokes?"

He smiled sheepishly. "Could I have two, please?"

I jumped up. "You got it. How was the yogi today?"

"Wonderful. He gave me a flower and taught me to meditate."

I opened the refrigerator. "Did you like it?"

"Yes. I got so relaxed I almost went to sleep. But he said that was OK." He paused, frowning in the direction of the bedroom. "Is Peter mad at me?"

"No. I told you, no one's mad. Would you like your Coke in a can or a glass?"

"I like it in a can. How come Peter hasn't come out of the room?"

"He's tired." So far Roger was wisely staying put. "He's resting."

"What time is it?"

"I don't know. Around ten. Maybe a little later."

"It's that late?"

"Yes," I lied.

"I didn't think Peter would be home. He said he was going to the yogi's evening meeting. That's what he told me when he dropped me off."

"Really? I think he did go." I returned to Jacob with the Cokes, both opened. "He just got home a few minutes ago."

"If he's not asleep yet, could I speak to him? I want to tell him I'm sorry."

I giggled again. Boy, I sounded guilty. "You don't have to tell him anything. It's better to drop it. Trust me on this. He won't want to talk about it." I lowered my voice, speaking confidentially. "It would just embarrass him."

Jacob was uncertain. "OK, I won't say anything. As long as he doesn't want to kick me out."

I gave Jacob a quick squeeze. "No one's going to kick you out. I told you last night, you can stay as long as you want. Now drink your Cokes and stop worrying. Oh, maybe you should change out of your swimming trunks first. You don't want to get the couch all wet."

Jacob felt his trunks. "They're dry from the sauna."

"Yeah, but you should probably still change. Here, let me help you into the bathroom. I got your sweats here. You can change and be all ready for bed." I helped him up.

"Do I have to go to bed now? Can't I watch TV?"

Jacob enjoyed several shows, and knew many TV characters well, even though he had trouble following action scenes. "Sure," I said. "You can watch whatever you want. I just think you should get ready for bed."

"OK."

The moment I had the bathroom door closed, I gestured to Roger. He was no fool. He was already dressed and ready to go. We had driven to the apartment in our own cars. He kissed me quickly as he headed out the door.

"Do I get a rain check?" he whispered.

"We'll see."

"Did you have fun?"

"Yes! Now go! Shoo!"

Roger grinned, enjoying my discomfort. "Do you love me?"

"Do you love me?" I asked.

He snorted. "I love what you do for me."

I pushed him away. "Get out of here!"

Jacob came out of the bathroom a few minutes later. He had changed and used the bathroom and brushed his teeth. With a dread bordering on nausea, I tried to think what he would say when Peter came rolling through the front door in a couple of hours. I could only hope Jacob was sound asleep by then. But even if he was, surely he would wake when his hero came home. Hey, Peter, I thought you were asleep in the bedroom. I could just see it now. What was I going to do?

"Hey, Jacob," I said. "Are you tired?"

"A little. Do I have to go to bed?"

"No. In fact, I was just thinking we should go to Disneyland."

"Disneyland? Right now?"

"Yes. Have you ever been to Disneyland?"

"No."

"It's great."

"But you want to go now?"

"Yes. What's wrong with now?"

"I thought you wanted me to get ready for bed?"

"Yeah, but you said you're not tired. So we should go to Disneyland."

"Is it open at this time?"

"Yeah. It's only nine o'clock."

"I thought you said it was ten o'clock?"

"I was wrong. I think, in the summer, Disneyland stays open late." I patted Jacob on the back. "Come on, you'll love it."

Jacob finally smiled. "Let's go."

Of course, I wanted to keep Jacob out long enough so Peter would be asleep when we came home. By tomorrow morning, I hoped, Jacob would have forgotten all about walking in on us.

Disneyland was crowded. It was a weekend night

in the summer, and a warm evening to boot. The line for Space Mountain was the longest but we went on it three times because the fun of it wasn't affected by whether you could see or not. In fact, each time I rode it, I kept my eyes clenched shut. Jacob howled; he was having the time of his life. We also went on the train ride because Jacob liked trains, and Thunder Mountain, which was another roller coaster-like ride. Jacob ate four hot dogs and two bags of popcorn and one slice of pizza. No stomach problems with this guy.

We got home at two in the morning and Peter was still up.

He glowed, I swear. I was jealous. Like the two preceding nights, he sat under the lamp in the corner reading. I had left him a note saying that I was taking Jacob to Disneyland, and that he shouldn't wait up for us. He smiled happily as we came through the door. Kriya and meditation obviously agreed with him.

"How was it?" he asked.

Jacob was still shaking with excitement. "Awesome! We went on every ride!"

I hadn't explained to Jacob that there was only one Space Mountain. I just gave it a new name each time. Leaning over to give Peter a kiss, I said, "It was a blast. How's the course going? Or do I need to ask?"

Peter nodded. "It's everything we hoped for. First we did some simple breathing exercises, then he taught us the kriya. During it you repeat certain set rhythms of breathing. Each rhythm is supposed to correspond to a different level: one to the body, one to the mind, another to the soul. The kriya integrates the different levels. I know that sounds abstract, but what it all boils down to is that after you do it, you feel incredible. You go really deep inside and when you come out it's like everything is brand-new. All your stress is gone and you feel like a little kid. You just want to play and have fun and enjoy life. It's amazing, you have to do it."

"I want to do it," I said honestly. I could have used a little less stress in my life. Especially when Jacob spoke next.

"Hey, Pete," he said. "I thought you were tired. I thought you went to bed early."

Peter was confused. "No. I went to the yogi's evening meeting. I told you I was going there when I dropped you off. Remember?"

"Yeah," Jacob said, "but when you came home you went to bed."

"Well," I broke in. "We don't know how long he's been home. It doesn't matter. Let's all go to bed. We all have to get up early tomorrow. Jacob, let me get your sweats for you. Here, I'll lead you to the bathroom. Peter, do you need anything?"

He still seemed a little puzzled. "No. I'm fine."

We were in bed ten minutes—Peter was already beginning to doze—when I spoke. There was no way I could sleep if I didn't. And I knew there would be no easy rest for me after I did, but that was the consequence of the choice I had made.

"Peter," I said softly.

"Huh?" he mumbled, his back to me.

"Roger was here this evening."

"What?"

"Roger was here this evening."

Peter rolled over and looked at me. "What are you talking about?"

I continued to stare at the ceiling, wishing I could leave my body, and soar through the roof and come once again to a place where there was no pain. I cleared my throat.

"Roger was here this evening."

"I heard you the first time. Why was he here?"

I swallowed. "I don't know."

"Shari?"

Tears formed in my eyes. "He was here with me. He was here when Jacob walked in. He was here and we were— We were here together, in this bed."

There was a long painful silence. Peter's voice came out like a croak.

"Why?"

I sat up and bent over, feeling as if I would vomit. Burying my face in my knees, I started to shake. "I'm sorry," I mumbled.

"Shari?"

"Yes."

His voice cracked. "Did you sleep with him?"

"Peter."

"Did you sleep with him?"

I sat up and looked over. His face was a burnt-out star.

"Almost," I said.

He died then, a little. I believe we both did. Certainly I felt like a murderer. He couldn't speak, he could scarcely breathe. I wanted to touch him, to comfort him. I tried, but he shook my hand off and I quickly withdrew it, knowing how my touch must feel to him. Like the skin of a rattler pulled across his skin. I turned away and put my feet on the floor, wondering if I had the strength to stand.

"I'm sorry," I told the wall.

He didn't speak. He only wept.

"Do you want me to leave?" I asked.

He didn't answer. His tears said it all.

I stood, swaying. "I think I should leave."

I dressed and packed an overnight bag and grabbed my notebook computer, slipping the floppy disk from my other computer into the notebook. Peter sat hugging his lifeless legs the whole time, forcing air into his lungs, awash in tears that burned both our souls. There were a million things I could have said to him. I was a writer and a genius at inventing lines of dialogue. Yet there was nothing to say now that would make things better. There comes a time, I suppose, when words fail. Love knows no reason, the yogi said. If that was true, I thought, then pain knew no answer. My pain was like a cancer, a disease I had freely chosen to share. How much I hated myself then was matched only by how little I understood myself. Above all else, I wished I had never been reborn.

I stepped to the bedroom door. On the living room couch, Jacob continued to sleep peacefully. Turning, I looked back at Peter, my dearest love.

"Goodbye," I said.

He didn't look up. "Goodbye."

I love you. More than anything in the whole creation, I love you.

"Take care of yourself, Peter," I whispered.

Then I was gone, into the night, where everything was and always would be black.

CHAPTER
XIII

*T*HE LOBBY OF THE Beverly Hills Hotel was plush. For a thousand bucks a night, it should have been. The guy at the desk took one look at me and was obviously inclined to point me in the direction of Motel 6. Without a spot of makeup and on the verge of a nervous breakdown, I was no sight for sore eyes. But when I pulled out my platinum American Express card his expression changed. The card had no limit. I didn't ask him for the room number of Roger Teller, or even if he could ring him for me. For the first time in a long time, I wasn't in the mood for sex and didn't even know why I had chosen to stay at that particular hotel.

My room was lovely. There were flowers on the coffee table and champagne on ice. The bathroom was as large as the egos of most people who probably stayed in the suite. I sampled the expensive Swiss chocolates that had been laid out for me, finding them tasteless. The champagne also tasted like vinegar. I spat it out after the first sip.

"Jesus," I whispered.

I got ready for bed. Turned out the lights. It didn't help. Sleep was not on good terms with broken hearts. It would have nothing to do with them. Thirty minutes later I was back up and turning on my notebook computer. If I couldn't rest, I decided, I'd work. Telling stories, lies, was the only thing I was good for.

THE STARLIGHT CRYSTAL

An hour after disabling the Orion vessel and deciding to flee—sixty minutes before Sarteen's starship would be in position to jump into hyperspace—the alien ship began to accelerate in their direction again. Pareen gave Sarteen the bad news.

"Captain," he said anxiously. "They're coming."

"Will they get to us before we jump?" she asked, sitting in her command chair on the bridge.

"It will be very close, one way or the other. But if I were to guess— Yes, they will just catch us."

Sarteen nodded to herself. She had erred. She should have fired the disrupters when she had the chance. Captain Eworl was probably laughing at her now. The extent of her mistake weighed heavily on her.

"Do we have any nanoeggs left?" she asked.

"I released our entire stock." Pareen shrugged. "I thought it was our last chance."

She gave him a reassuring smile. "I understand. I would have released them all as well. Now, what do we do? We must assume they'll catch up to us. They are

151

damaged, and perhaps their shields aren't working. Can we defeat them in a direct fight?"

Pareen shook his head. "Doubtful. They only need to hit us once with their energy beams. I cannot believe we destroyed all their weaponry."

"By your best estimate, how close will we come to having sufficient velocity to jump into hyperspace?" she asked.

"We will have ninety-eight percent of required velocity."

"What if we implode our engines? Just as they come within firing range?"

Pareen was aghast. "That will permanently destroy our engines. When we come out of hyperspace on the other side we won't be able to slow."

"We can decelerate using our retro rockets."

"That'll take years."

"Will we be in a hurry? We have already spent a thousand years aboard this ship. What are a few more? If we implode the engines that will give us the last shove we need to jump into hyperspace."

"Are you forgetting that we already have serious structural damage? The implosion will probably destroy us."

"It is a chance we'll have to take since it is our only chance." Sarteen stood. "I am going to my quarters. I will be back in time for our jump."

Once more Sarteen turned to her golden column of precious stones for guidance. Its proximity soothed her, brought her into a state of calm clarity and intuition where she felt as if she could almost touch the great secrets of the universe to understand the reason for this attack. Yet in her heart she felt she already knew the answer to the riddle. The invasion had occurred because, as a people, they were not ready to be with the Elders. And even the Elders had not known that. Perhaps in their great love for humanity, they had reached out too soon to bring their children home. Perhaps the Elders, too, were under attack. That was a disturbing thought. Yet Sarteen somehow doubted that that was the case. The Orions were physical, the Elders interdimensional. The Elders could not be fenced in as Earth could be. Sarteen had tried repeatedly to contact home, any of the planets, without success. Sadly, she felt there was no escape for them. Not in the foreseeable future.

"But we must escape," she said to the empty room. "We must live."

Even before speaking to Eworl, she had sensed the hatred of the Orions. Now that they'd had contact, there was no doubt in her mind that the enemy planned to turn Earth into a planet of pain. To gloat over when they grew angry or bored.

What could defeat these hideous creatures? Where was their vulnerable point? Before contact was lost with the galactic center, the Elders had explained that three feelings in the heart guided the destiny of all creatures: love, hatred, and fear. Clearly the Orions had hatred in abundance and seemed to have no use for love. But what about fear? Were they easily frightened? Could their captain be tricked—out of fear—into making a mistake? Perhaps she would get the chance to test the idea. The Elders had said where there was no love, fear always lurked close.

The communicator on her desk beeped.

"Yes?" she said.

"The Orion vessel is closing more rapidly than I thought possible."

"Will we still be able to implode the engines and get into hyperspace?"

"The farther we are from our desired velocity, the more difficult it will be. You'd better return to the bridge. Also, we have another problem, if it is a problem. The aliens have fixed a peculiar beam on us. It is not a weapon of any sort, not one that I am familiar with anyway. But it is causing minute changes in the hull of our ship."

"What kind of changes?"

"It is irradiating the hull—slightly. I'm puzzled because this level of radiation could not possibly harm us. It's more as if we are being marked."

"For what purpose?"

"I have no idea. But it makes me nervous."

Sarteen stood. "I am on my way."

On the bridge Pareen continued to analyze the energy beam from the Orion ship. Sarteen stood by his side as he worked. She had made the decision to implode the engines because it was, as she had said, their only chance. Her feeling on the matter had not changed, yet as the time of implosion approached, she grew anxious. Pareen was correct: implosion was dangerous with a sound ship, but with the deep gashes in the hull, it was doubly so. The procedure called for them to transform their engines into the equivalent of a huge bomb, which would give them an extra kick in velocity as it was spent. The trouble was that sometimes an implosion could go out of control and annihilate everything in the immediate vicinity. In her youth, centuries ago, Sarteen had witnessed a starship that had been forced to implode its engines. It had not survived.

"Are you certain their beam is not harming us?" Sarteen asked.

"It isn't. As I said, it just seems to be marking us. Perhaps they use it before firing their weapons, to get a better fix on us."

"I don't think so. They had no trouble getting a fix on us last time. I want to implode the engines now, and take our chances."

"I advise against it," Pareen said. "The closer we are to light velocity, the greater chance we'll have of surviving the jump into hyperspace."

"Another thirty minutes of acceleration will make little difference. Also, we don't know the actual range of their weapons."

"Last time they waited until they were close before they opened fire," Pareen said.

Sarteen stepped away, toward her seat. "It means nothing. Prepare the engines for implosion. Alert all decks. It will be a rough ride."

"It may be a short ride," Pareen said grimly.

A few minutes later, just as the Orion ship came into view, they were set for their big gamble. Under maximum magnification, it still looked seriously damaged. Yet Sarteen noticed another weapons port on the far side, steadily increasing its energy discharge; an angry red eye in the black well of space. Wary of another trick, Captain Eworl was preparing to attack from a distance. Let him try firing over hundreds of light-years, Sarteen thought. If the implosion worked, they'd be that far from the solar system in a matter of seconds.

"What is our destination?" Pareen asked.

"The Pleiades star cluster," Sarteen said, having made the decision earlier. There were numerous planets in that particular system capable of supporting life. Plus Pleiadian skies, filled with hundreds of blue stars floating in rivers of nebulae, were glorious. A fitting heaven to give the children of humanity. Pareen nodded at her choice, approving.

"We are ready," he said a minute later, sitting down and fastening his seat belt.

"What are our chances?" Sarteen asked.

"Less than one in three."

"If we don't make it, I want it to go on the official record that you opposed this idea. That way history will say you should have been the captain."

"You are clever," Pareen said. "History will only have a chance to read the record if you're right. Let's leave our last entry blank. That way we're both wrong—or right."

Sarteen smiled. "Agreed." She sat back in her chair and fastened her belt. "Initiate implosion."

Her command was obeyed. Unlike when they were struck with the Orion energy beam, the ship did not convulse with shock waves. The *Crystal* had a dampening field around it that kept their frail human bodies from being crushed while they were under acceleration. Obviously, with the implosion of their engines, the increase in acceleration was dramatic, yet even that pressure was cancelled out by the field. Nevertheless, Sarteen felt terrific *internal* motion when Pareen pusned the button. It was as if her consciousness was momentarily split open, and it was able to extend in two separate directions. Her body hummed; every cell could have suddenly begun vibrating at a high rate. She had closed her eyes and therefore could not be sure if the lights failed. Yet inside everything went black. And cold—it was an eerie sensation to feel as if she had been dropped into a galactic vortex, a whirlwind of colliding forces, that spun around and around and never reached bottom. It was like being dead; at least, what she would have imagined nonexistence to be. How long she remained in that state, she didn't know. Out of nowhere Pareen was shouting something important.

"We have made the jump! We are outside the Pleiades!"

Sarteen opened her eyes, seeing the blazing blue splendor of the cluster on the main viewing screen.

She smiled. "Thank God."

"Don't thank anybody too soon!" Pareen cried. "The Orions have made the jump, too!"

Sarteen leaped to her feet. "That's impossible. Nothing can track a ship through hyperspace."

Pareen shook his head. "Now we know why they were irradiating our hull. That radiation must have left a trail of our jump. Their technology is even more advanced than we imagined."

"How far behind us are they?" Sarteen asked.

"Two minutes."

"Can we maneuver? Fire weapons?"

"No. We're dead in space, drifting. Our engines are gone. We have to surrender."

"We will not surrender!" Sarteen shouted.

"Then we will die, this time without a fight." Pareen consulted his instruments. "They are energizing their weapons."

Sarteen thought frantically. Their weak spot must be fear; the clarity bestowed on her by the golden column would not have misled her. Yet how could she frighten them when she had only minutes to live? Or was she asking the question backward? If fear was their blind spot, would they not assume it was humanity's weakness as well? How could she make it appear that they—her crew and herself—were helpless because of fear?

"We will go to Parting mode," she said.

Parting, as they called it, involved separating the living quarters of the ship from the control and power sections. The living quarters could slip off from the spherical *Crystal* like pieces of a sliced fruit. Lacking contact with the main engines, the sections could scarcely maneuver, and certainly could not fight. Yet, with the help of retro rockets, they would still be able to steer toward an Earth-like planet—and take fifty years to get there. It was better than going up in a ball of flame. But as Pareen's stunned expression said, what was the point of executing a Parting? The Orions would just blow the other sections out of the ether.

"Why bother?" Pareen asked. "Shouldn't we die together?"

Sarteen shook her head. "Their captain must be able to see we are helpless. If we initiate Parting, he may bring his ship in close." She nodded to Pareen. "Clear the bridge. Notify the remainder of the crew. I alone will stay to greet this Eworl."

"Wait," Pareen said.

"Do it! We don't have time for argument."

"I merely wanted to ask permission to stay with you."

Sarteen smiled as she sat back down. "Permission granted. After Parting is complete—and assuming we're still alive—I want you to go to the lab and get a nanoegg and bring it to the bridge. Attach it to the communication board. Rig it to explode on my voice command."

"But I told you—we have no nanoeggs left."

"You forget our experimental original. It is not spaceworthy, and contains only typical antimatter, not the condensed version. But it will still do nicely as a self-destruct weapon."

"Why not just self-destruct now?" Pareen asked.

Sarteen leaned forward, studying the screen and the approaching alien ship. "This Captain Eworl will want to gloat over his prey before destroying it. That will be his style, I think. But he may make a mistake and come too close." She glanced over at Pareen. "Are you sure you want to stay with me?"

He didn't hesitate. "It will be my honor to die by your side."

Her plan was built on several factors. She had explained some but not all the details to Pareen. Because the *Crystal*'s weapon systems and engines were as good as dead, Eworl would see her vessel as harmless. Yet if he were human, he would not bring his ship close enough to be destroyed by a self-destruct command on her part. Nevertheless, that was her hope, and she didn't believe it a vain hope. Because Captain Eworl was *not* human. He was the product of a hateful race, a race that probably cared as little for its own members as it did for those of another race. It was possible he could not conceive of an act of total sacrifice; that she should stay behind and give up her life to save the lives of her crew. Also, as she had said to Pareen, he might want to take captives, to take her prisoner. To have her stand by his side while he wiped out the remaining sections of her ship. Yes, she thought, he would enjoy that. He would not start the killing until he had her.

But he would never have her.

Together, Pareen and Sarteen watched as the four living quarter sections of the *Crystal* fired their retro rockets and plowed away. Each section was self-contained; her people could survive in space for centuries if need be. If it took that long to reach a life-sustaining world. Silently, she wished them good luck. Beside her, Pareen shook his head.

"If they do survive," he said. "Will their descendants remember this day?"

"It will take only one to remember," Sarteen said thoughtfully, again feeling the sensation she had experienced during the hyperjump. As if she were in two places at one time, in two minds. Shaking herself, she turned back to her seat. "Put the Orion ship on the screen. Hail their captain."

Pareen turned to obey. "He won't believe anything you have to say."

She sat down with a sigh. "He doesn't have to believe

me. He just has to want something from me. Are their weapons still energized?"

"Yes. They have us in their sights. Hailing frequencies open."

"Captain Eworl," she said pleasantly. "We await your instructions."

Once again they received only audio, no video, from their pursuers. The alien captain did not sound as if he were in a good mood. "Prepare for boarding."

Sarteen winked at Pareen. "Our docking bays are open and ready. Do you require special atmospheric conditions?"

"Negative. Disarm and prepare to be taken captive." Captain Eworl paused. "We will tolerate no further deception."

"Understood. Our surrender is total and unconditional. We await your arrival." Sarteen made a motion to Pareen to cut the signal. "The beast falls for the bait," she muttered.

"I'm surprised. I thought he would have been more careful."

Sarteen continued to stare at the approaching Orion ship. Its purple taloned fin, its glowing weapons ports— they reminded her of a nightmare of a half-seen monster she faintly remembered having had. Maybe the recurring dream was the reason she knew mankind's day of rejoicing had not yet arrived. Maybe it was something else. Something older.

"I'm not surprised," she said. "Victory is hollow without the spoils of war. For him to merely destroy us is not enough. He has to bring something back to show his comrades. A trophy to place on his shelf." She nodded to herself. "He wants me."

The Orion vessel, the *Adharma*, docked a short time afterward. At that instant Sarteen's plot could have borne fruit. She could have ignited the nanoegg implanted beneath the bridge communication board, and blown both ships to dust. Impatient, Pareen awaited the command but she shook her head. No, wait, she said. We will wait. Here, at the end, was she suddenly afraid to die? Did she honestly believe that there was a hope of escape? To these questions she had no answers. Yet she knew she needed to confront the enemy. To look into his face, his eyes, and see whether she had seen him before.

"And whether I will see him again," she whispered.

"What did you say?" Pareen asked.

"Nothing. Are their airlocks compatible with ours?"

Pareen checked his instruments. "Apparently. Several of them have already entered the lock. There are six of them. They are pressurizing the chamber." He paused. "They'll reach the bridge in two minutes."

"Have you set the nanoegg to explode on my voice command?"

"Not yet. What word would you like to use as the trigger?"

"The word *Cira.*"

"Why that word?"

Sarteen smiled sadly. "Did you know I had a daughter?"

"You never told me."

"It was many years ago. Her name is Cira. Was Cira." She added softly, "She lived on Malanak, the fifth planet."

Pareen was sympathetic. "I'm sorry."

Sarteen sighed. "At least it ended quickly for her. That's why this captain lets us live this long. He wants our end to be painful. It's pain that feeds him."

"How do you know that?" Pareen asked, working his instruments.

"You will understand when you see him."

"Surely the captain will not be a member of the boarding team."

Sarteen shrugged. "Why not? He thinks we're help-less. He can't imagine we would intentionally kill our-selves. He can't imagine an existence beyond the body. You know, that's what this is all about. The Orions don't believe we have souls." She paused. "Maybe *they* don't."

"Don't say your daughter's name again unless you want the nanoegg detonated."

"Understood. Where are they now?"

"Coming up the elevator." He pointed to the door at the rear of the bridge. "They will come through there."

Sarteen stood, faced the elevator. "How long?"

"One minute. Maybe less."

Sarteen gestured for him to stand beside her. "Pareen," she said. "This last thousand years, has it ever bothered you that I was the captain and not you? We're about to die. You can tell me the truth."

He came close. "Yes. Many times. When I disagreed

with you. But at each of those times I later saw the wisdom of your decisions." He nodded toward the elevator door. "This plan was clever. We can stop them now. The others will escape."

"If I say my daughter's name."

"I believe that would be the wise thing to do."

She put an arm around him. "Trust me this last time, Pareen. I won't let you down."

"I trust you, Sarteen."

She leaned over and kissed his cheek. "They have taken the Earth, but it does not belong to them. Let's make a vow to each other. If we are ever given the chance—in whatever time, whatever place—to get the Earth back, we will give it our whole heart. We will not rest until our home is returned to us."

"Agreed." Pareen paused and stared into her eyes. "Did I ever tell you how I feel about you, Sarteen?"

She smiled sadly. "No. Did I ever tell you?"

"No." He glanced at the elevator. "And now there's no time."

She hugged him again. "There's time."

But maybe she was wrong.

At that moment the elevator door opened.

"What does Eworl look like?" I asked my computer screen. "How does Sarteen trick him? How does she get out of this mess?"

Word processors were great inventions. They allowed you to cut and paste and delete and replace. But they could not write your books for you. Certainly they could not help you with your own life. The questions I asked—I wondered if they were for Sarteen or for myself. I felt a deep kinship with her—the whole universe was tumbling down on both our heads.

Turning off the machine, I went to bed.

I slept, a little. There were no dreams.

CHAPTER

XIV

THE FOLLOWING AFTERNOON, Sunday, after shooting another wet scene as Mary, Garrett agreed to
meet me in his office on my lunch hour. Mary was
also in the scenes that were to be shot that afternoon and evening; I had only a few minutes to
spare, but I had asked him to meet me in person,
rather than talk to me on the phone because I
wanted an excuse to leave the set. After coming so
close to having sex with Roger the previous night, I
found it difficult to act casual around him. I was
ashamed and in lust at the same time. He kept
smiling at me; it was unnerving.

Garrett offered me coffee, which I refused. He
came straight to the point.

"You were right when you said Roger Teller was
an elusive guy," he said. "I ran into problems with
something as simple as the DMV check on his car."

"What kind of problems?"

"It turned up nothing."

"What does that mean?"

"His license plate is phony. Assuming you wrote down the number correctly."

"I gave you the right number. How could he have a phony license plate?"

Garrett shrugged. "It's not hard to make a fake license plate, if you're so inclined. It's just that I've never met anyone who went to the trouble."

"*Why* would he have a phony license plate?" I asked.

"To prevent someone from checking up on him, and it worked. It was a dead end for me. So I decided to check into his past acting jobs."

"They also turned out to be fake?"

"No. Each of the places he said he'd been, he really had been. The two acting classes he took, the three plays he was in were genuine. What was curious was how the people in those places talked about him."

"Go on," I said, my curiosity sparked.

"Let me tell you what his last acting teacher, a Mr. Hatcher, said. This Hatcher was on a sci-fi TV series a few years ago. He was, and is, a pretty good actor. Anyway, Hatcher runs a workshop where actors write one-act scripts alone or in pairs and then act them out with a partner in front of the class. Being a producer, I assume you're familiar with the format. By the final class, everyone in the workshop—except Roger and his partner—had done their scenes. Roger was determined to be last. He had gone out of his way to chose the most beautiful young woman in the group as his partner. Hatcher said she seemed very sensible when she joined the workshop. Yet when Roger performed his scene with her, Hatcher had doubts."

"Why?" I asked.

"In front of a class of approximately thirty people, Roger and the girl did a scene where he simulated raping her and stabbing her in the leg, before finally befriending her."

I frowned. "I don't see how that would work."

Garrett snorted. "It's not a question of whether it would work. It's disgusting!"

I nodded. "I understand that. But you don't work in Hollywood. There are rape scenes on prime time TV. That he wrote and performed such a scene is odd, but it doesn't mean he's disturbed."

Garrett stared at her. "I don't think I would fit in in Hollywood very well."

I shrugged. "On a clear day you can see the city out the window of your office. What did the other people say about him?"

"Hatcher gave me a list of people who had taken the workshop. So far, I've been unable to reach the young woman who worked with Roger on the scene. But I did talk to a guy who occasionally went out drinking with him afterward. They would go to a nearby bar and stay out late. Roger, the guy said, could really put them away."

"So? Lots of people drink."

"You asked me to check up on him. To a detective, this is significant. The guy drinks a lot. Not only that, the man I spoke to said he never saw Roger drunk."

"Yes? Am I missing something?"

Garrett scratched his head. "I don't know. I don't even know why I'm telling you this. Except the guy I spoke to—he found Roger's tolerance amazing. He said Roger could put away two bottles of wine and six beers and be perfectly sober." Garrett paused. "Have you seen him drink on the set?"

I hesitated. "Not on the set. But afterward."

Garrett consulted his notes. "Next I spoke to the director of a play Roger was in called *Summer Sleep*. Are you familiar with the story? A woman by the name of Annette Ginger wrote it at the turn of the century. She's not well known nowadays, but in her time she was considered brilliant."

"I'm afraid I've never heard of her."

"Summer Sleep is a murder mystery. A group of young men and women travel to a large mansion in upstate New York. There's the usual big storm to isolate them from the rest of the world, and the typical history about how people have died in the mansion under strange circumstances. Yet the mystery is unique; it goes in unexpected directions. Roger played the role of the villain, who was in reality the grandchild of one of the mansion's original victims. It will take me too long to explain the whole story but suffice it to say the role is a demanding one because it requires the actor to be the obvious suspect from the beginning, yet disarm the audience with his innocence. The character does and says one thing after another that incrimi-

nates himself. Yet the way Ms. Ginger wrote the play, if the actor can pull it off, he can stun the audience."

"Because his guilt is so obvious he couldn't possibly have committed the crime?"

"Exactly. You should read the play. You'd enjoy it."

"I'll see if I can find a copy of it." I paused. "How did Roger do in the role?"

"Excellent. The Chicago *Herald* reviewed him. It said he was someone to keep an eye on. The only trouble was the play closed after opening night."

"Why?"

"The actress who played the heroine got beat up."

I grimaced. "How bad?"

"Her jaw was broken. She was cut on her cheek. The director said the wound took twenty stitches to close. Something like that would scar, I'd think. I know the question you want to ask. Was Roger responsible for what happened to her? The police say no, although Roger was taken in for questioning. The girl herself never said it was Roger."

"Then why are you building this up to make it seem it might have been Roger?"

"Because the director thought it might have been him."

"Did he have any proof?"

"No hard proof. But I find it strange that a director who worked daily with an actor would suspect him of such a heinous crime. You see, Roger was involved with this young lady. They were living together. And the police report on the crime does state that the girl refused to cooperate with the police in apprehending the criminal."

"Why would the girl protect Roger if he had hurt her so badly? It makes no sense."

"Why would she refuse to cooperate with the authorities if she wasn't protecting someone? Sometimes you have to ask the question backward to arrive at the real question. I had a case a few years ago—when I was still with the police force—where everyone thought a seventeen-year-old girl had committed suicide by jumping off a balcony. On purely circumstantial evidence, even her friends assumed the girl had killed herself. Yet, at the time, I kept asking myself, why would she have done such a thing? She had her whole life in front of her. And until someone could prove to me that she wanted to die, I proceeded on the assumption that she had been murdered. Turned out I was right. Oh, by the way, you might have heard of the girl. Her name was Shari Cooper—the same as your pen name."

I had to remember to breathe. "You know who I am?"

"Yes," he said casually. "You're the writer."

"Have you been checking up on me as well, Mr. Garrett?"

He snorted. "Hardly. My daughter has read a couple of your books. I mentioned to her that you were the producer on a movie called *First to Die* and she got all excited. I guess it's one of her favorite books. Since you told me you were president of Cooper Productions, I put two and two together." He paused, uncertain. "You are Shari Cooper, aren't you?"

I smiled faintly. "I'm Jean Rodrigues. But I would be happy to sign a book for your daughter, if she wishes." God, I thought. It had been madness to come to this office. I continued. "It seems to me you're condemning Roger on purely circumstantial evidence. The same way this Shari Cooper's friends did."

Garrett watched me closely. Somehow, I had pushed a button in him, not a wise move. I had to remind myself how shrewd he was; how he could take the obvious, and see the hidden motive behind it. He had caught Amanda easily enough, thank God. She was another person I had to look up someday, when I was feeling reckless. I wondered if she was still locked away. I never talked to Jimmy about her. The subject pained him too much. Garrett took his time responding.

"You misunderstand me," he said. "I'm not out to condemn Roger. I'm impartial. He's your employee, not mine. You have to work with him on a daily basis. Once again, you hired me to find out these things I'm telling you. For that reason, I must in good conscience offer you my personal evaluation of what I've uncovered. Already I see a pattern here. You may not recognize it, but I do. Roger Teller is a young man who uses young women. I don't care how fanatical you are about your art. You don't write a scene about rape and stabbing and play it out in front of people unless you have serious emotional problems. And you don't beat up your girlfriend and simultaneously scare her so badly that she's afraid to talk to the police." He added, "Not unless you have serious emotional problems."

"Why do you assume he hurt her? I don't get it?"

"Why do you assume he didn't?" Garrett paused. "Unless you're personally involved with him."

I stiffened. "My personal business is just that— personal. I don't pay you to pry into it. Have you anything else to tell me?"

Garrett was unmoved by my rebuff. President of a production company or not, I was still just a punk kid to him. "Nothing new. Just a reminder that two separate men—an accomplished actor and a re-spected director—did not like Roger Teller. They didn't trust him, and I don't think you should trust him either. Not a guy who goes to the trouble to manufacture a phony license plate."

"I will take your advice under consideration. What about Roger's family? His source of income?"

"I'm still looking into that. I have a buddy who works for the Chicago Police. He's supposed to get back to me by tomorrow. He said he had a lead on Roger Teller that might prove interesting."

"Could you elaborate?"

Garrett shook his head. "He refused to elaborate. He wanted to check it out first. That's a cop for you. But this guy's good. He won't go running all over town wasting your money."

"Am I paying him as well?"

173

Garrett smiled. "Indirectly. I'm sorry if I was heavy-handed a moment ago. It comes with the job. Hey, there's a question I wanted to ask you."

I forced a chuckle. "Where do I get my ideas?"

"Yeah. Does everyone ask you that?"

I stood. "Ninety-nine percent of people. The truth is, I get them in the strangest places. You have no idea how strange. May I see you tomorrow at this time?"

He stood up to walk me out. "Yes, that would be fine. My Chicago buddy should have reported in by then. Oh, if it wouldn't be too much trouble, my daughter left a copy of one of your books on her desk for you to sign. It would mean a lot to her."

I smiled again. "No problem. I'll be glad to sign it."

Garrett followed me into the reception area. Because it was Sunday, his daughter had the day off or else was at lunch. I had eaten nothing all day, but wasn't hungry. When you went to hell and back you didn't pack a lunch. Nothing worked as effectively as the pain and suffering diet. *Cry Those Calories Away.* I should write such a diet book and sell millions of copies.

Garrett's daughter had left a copy of *First to Die.* Quickly I scribbled my best wishes and name. Garrett took the book and held it as if it was worth its weight in gold. It never ceased to amaze me how much my sloppy signature meant to people. Yet as I was leaving, he made a remark that stopped me cold.

"Actually, she was hesitant to have you sign this book," he said.

"I don't understand?"

"She didn't want to impose on you twice. She wanted you to sign the other one."

I froze. "What other one?"

"Your new one. She was going to pick up a copy today at the mall. What's it called? *Remember Me?*"

I smiled thinly. "Tell her not to bother buying it. It's my worst book." Quickly I turned away. "Have a nice afternoon, Mr. Garrett."

"You too, Shari. I mean, Jean."

His slip of the tongue had been accidental. Nothing more.

But what about tomorrow?

CHAPTER

XV

*M*Y HEAD STARTED TO THROB the moment I set foot back on the set. I had no choice, I had to take two Tylenol-3. The pain medicine worked, yet I wasn't sure if the same could be said for my celluloid luster. That evening, watching the dailies, I thought I either had to rewrite Mary as a dope-smoking chick or else get a new actress to play my body double. My eyes were out of focus in every shot.

Roger, warm-blooded American boy that he was, wanted to take me to dinner and bed. But I begged off, telling him that I had a headache. He was sympathetic and didn't pressure me. I didn't tell him where I was staying.

When I reached my hotel suite, I called Peter. Hardest thing I ever had to do.

Harder than dying. I died a little when he answered and I heard the pain in his voice. "Hello?" he said.

"Peter, this is Shari. I'm so sorry."

There was a long pause. "Where are you?" he asked.

"At a hotel. By myself. How are you?"

He sighed. "Not so good."

"I'm sorry. I don't know how it happened."

I could hear him breathing. "Are you going to see him again?"

I knew he'd ask me that, of course. I tried to decide how I would respond. After the lies I'd put him through, the truth was all I could offer him now.

"I have to see him every day at the set. He's our star and we're stuck with him. At this point Henry won't let me make another change. But I don't plan to go out with him anymore. I don't want to do that. I didn't want to do it to begin with. I just did. He has some kind of hold on me—I can't explain it." I stopped. "I know that isn't exactly what you wanted to hear, but it's the best I can give you."

Peter moaned softly. "Are you sure you didn't have sex with him?"

"Yes, I'm sure. I'd remember, you know."

"Shari."

"I'm sorry," I said quickly. "That didn't come out the way I meant it. What I was trying to say is, it went too far. I crossed the line." I added, although it broke my heart to do so, "You have every right to leave me if you want."

Another long painful silence. "Do you want to leave me?"

"No. Not for anything in the world."

"Then how come you can't swear that you'll never see him again?"

I began to cry. "I don't know how come."

Peter pleaded. "Don't go to the movie set. They can make it without you. Henry's a genius. He's made dozens of movies. You're a writer—that's your gift. That's what you came back for—to tell stories. To inspire people. You don't need to be a producer or a director. Come back here to me. It can be like it was before. We've been happy, Shari. We belong together. Please?"

I sobbed. "I can't!"

He wept with me. "Why not? What's stopping you?"

"I don't deserve you!"

"Shari."

"I betrayed you! I might betray you again!"

He lowered his voice. "Is it the sex thing? Is that what you need?"

"It's more complicated than that. I feel I have to confront . . ." My voice trailed off.

"Confront what?"

I paused, feeling cold. The words had just come out of my mouth. "I don't know—the unreal maybe."

"What's the *unreal?*"

I spoke as if I were suddenly far away. On a spaceship, light-years from Earth. "Everything that isn't real." My mind felt split then as Sarteen's had when she leaped through the uncharted region of hyperspace. Indeed, I felt very close to her then. As if our mutual dilemmas were simply two sides of the same coin. Yet I did not understand what my affinity with a fictional character meant any more than I knew how to end that story. "The Starlight Crystal"—why had I called it that? In reference to the crystals in her golden column? The precious jewels that vibrated with my heroine's chakras? I remembered how my forehead and heart had vibrated in the company of the yogi.

"Shari?" Peter said, confused. Some time must have gone by.

"How's your course?" I asked. "Did you complete it today?"

"Yes. It was wonderful. It kept me from jumping off a balcony."

"Or driving head on into a truck?"

He was sad. "Yeah."

"That was a sick joke. I'm sorry."

"Mine was, too. I guess we're both sorry."

"How's the yogi?" I asked.

"Wonderful." Peter hesitated. "I told him what was happening between us."

"That's OK. I'm sure he knew anyway."

"As a matter of fact he did. He said it was inevitable."

I didn't know if I liked the sound of that. "What does that mean?"

"He said this situation was all set up by nature, and by ourselves. That we test ourselves."

I forced a chuckle. "Did he say I was failing the test?"

"I asked him—"

"And?"

"He didn't answer. He doesn't always answer. It's his way."

I spoke with feeling. "I'd love to see him again."

"He wants to see you. He asked for you to come see him."

"I thought he was leaving."

"He decided to stay longer." Peter paused. "Please come home. We can go see him together. He can help us through this difficult time."

"I don't deserve his help."

"Shari! Why do you keep saying these crazy things?"

"It's not crazy. I didn't keep my end of the bargain. I don't know what that means either, but I know it's true." I paused. Someone was knocking at my door. "Peter, I have to go now."

"What is it? We need to talk more."

"We can talk later. I'll call you."

He sounded so pitiful. "You promise?"

"I promise. I love you, Peter. You have to believe that. Whatever happens, that will never change."

He sighed. "The yogi said I had to believe that."

The knock came again. "He's a wise man. Trust him. Take care of yourself."

"I love you, Shari."

I smiled, feeling the tears well up again. "I know you do. Try to relax. Goodbye."

Yet it was a false alarm, the knock at the door. The maid simply wanted to know if I needed fresh flowers. Sure, I said. I could sit and smell them all by myself. She arranged a silver vase with two dozen red roses on the mantle above the fireplace and then discreetly departed. Because of my vow not to call Roger, I had nothing to do except finish my story and rest. Certainly I didn't feel like going out and painting the town. But when I turned on my notebook computer, I discovered that my muse was off helping a college student write a term paper or something. I felt about as inspired as a crashed disk. Turning off my magical machine, I tried the TV, not a favorite pastime of mine. If I wanted to watch something, I usually rented a movie. The remote control had several buttons for pay TV. The bottom one on the left let you watch X-rated features. Briefly, I wondered what Roger was doing, if he was alone.

I won't call him. I won't see him. I love Peter.

I wondered what Garrett's buddy in Chicago would discover.

The night crept by. Fifty channels on TV and I couldn't find anything to watch. I took a bath. The hotel offered an assortment of expensive oils to pour in the water. Wanting to get my thousand-bucks-a-night's worth, I dumped them all in. Came out of the tub smelling like the vase above the fireplace. I blow-dried my hair and ordered a hot fudge sundae from room service—that was a smart move. Tasted yummy, even though I was on the second day of my pain and suffering diet. I had ordered a turkey sandwich as well, but it didn't appeal to me. But I could see how people grew addicted to staying at expensive hotels. You just had to pick up the phone and dial a number and life was taken care of for you. I probably could have ordered stronger pills for my headache. The pain was coming back. Playing with my bottle of pills, I wondered how I would look and feel in the morning if I swallowed another two before I went to bed. Probably like the cheerleader after the sharks got her.

It was ironic that I should think about sharks as I turned out the light.

The call came at two in the morning. Groaning, I rolled over and turned on the light. Earlier, as a compromise, I had taken only one pill before putting my head on the pillow. Unfortunately, the *pleasant* half of the medicine had already worn off. Now I had only side effects percolating in my system. As I sat up, a vein pounded at my right temple, and I felt hung over. Picking up the phone, I hoped it was a wrong number.

"Hello?" I mumbled.

"Shari, this is Bob. I'm down at the shark set. I've got to talk to you about tomorrow's scene."

"Now? Bob, it's the middle of the night. How did you get this number?"

"Henry gave it to me. You gave it to him. This is important, Shari. We have to talk."

I yawned. "All right, I'm awake. What do you want to talk about?"

"Not on the phone. You have to come down here."

"No way. Knowing you, you'll probably shove me in the water and I'd be eaten alive."

He lowered his voice. "It's funny you should say that. Someone is planning to do exactly that tomorrow."

"What are you talking about? Who?"

"This is not something we can discuss on the phone. Be here in forty minutes. I'll be waiting by the boat. Don't be late."

"Wait a second," I began. But he had already hung up. For the life of me, I couldn't understand why Henry would have given Bob my number. I had specifically told him to keep my whereabouts secret. Of course, he knew where Roger was staying and must have figured we were having a wild old time.

I don't know why I called Roger. I had told myself a million times that I wouldn't. I guess I just needed someone to bounce Bob's crazy conversation off. Roger answered after the fifth ring. He sounded dead to the world.

"Yeah?"

"Roger, this is Shari. I'm sorry to wake you. We have a problem. It's Bob."

He groaned. "What time is it?"

"Two in the morning. I wouldn't have disturbed you if I didn't think this was important. Bob called me a minute ago and said that someone plans to push one of our crew in the water with the sharks— while we're shooting tomorrow."

Roger snorted. "The entire cast has joked about pushing someone in the water with sharks. We all grew up with *Jaws*. It's nothing. Bob's pulling your leg. Go back to sleep."

"I'd like to. But there was something in his voice—I don't think he was joking. He wants me to meet him down by the shark set. I want you to come with me."

He paused. "Are you serious about this?"

"Yes. I can come get you in a few minutes."

"In a few minutes? Where are you?"

I bit my lower lip. "I'm staying here, in your hotel."

"Shari. Why didn't you tell me that?"

"I'll explain when I see you. Get dressed. We have to see what Bob wants. Something's happening here that I don't understand."

Roger yawned. "You're not the only one."

CHAPTER
XVI

ON THE WAY TO SEE BOB, sitting in the passenger seat of Roger's black Corvette, I explained to Roger that Peter and I were having difficulties but that they were unrelated to what had happened between us. Roger nodded and didn't press me for details. He was remarkably cool about the whole thing. He even confessed to feeling guilty about moving in on me while I was living with Peter. Yet, grinning, he added that he wasn't losing any sleep over it.

"I was sleeping fine until you called," he said. "You know, Bob's going to laugh when he sees how he managed to get us out of bed. In fact, I wouldn't be surprised if he's not even there."

"Whatever happens, don't get in a fight with him around the sharks."

"I know I have a temper. I'll watch it." He paused. "Tell me about the story you're working on?"

"Did I tell you that I was writing a story?"

"You write for a living. I assume you're always working on a story."

"Not always. I think a gap between stories is important. It allows what's inside to ripen. That's my take on the creative process anyway. Actually, though, I am working on a short story called 'The Starlight Crystal.' It's sci-fi—it takes place in the future."

Roger lowered the radio. "Tell me about it."

"Now? It's so late. Let me tell you another time."

"No. I want to hear it, honestly. I told you, your stories affect me deeply."

He sure knew the way to a writer's heart. Tell an author he or she is a genius and he or she will give you the world in exchange. "I probably should tell you," I said. "You're the one who inspired the story."

"Really? How?"

"A few nights ago I had a dream where I was flying around the city, visiting people I knew, putting my hands on them and entering their dreams."

Roger watched me. "The girl in your latest book did that. When she was dead."

I had forgotten that he had read *Remember Me.* That book haunted me everywhere I turned. I spoke hastily. "That's probably why I dreamed it. Anyway, in the dream I visited you and put my hands on your head. And you were dreaming about a great interstellar battle. Humanity versus the invading aliens." I paused, wanting to ask a question.

"Do you remember the dream, Roger?"

But it was too peculiar a thing to say. Especially since I was supposed to be unrelated to the Shari Cooper in my book.

"It sounds neat," Roger said. "What do the aliens look like?"

"I don't know."

"How much of this story have you written?"

"It's almost done."

"And you don't know what the aliens look like?"

"No. I have no idea."

"Who wins in the end? Humanity or the aliens?"

"I don't know."

Roger acted exasperated. "Tell me what you *do* have."

I did as he requested, starting with Sarteen and Pareen's journey home, to the moment when Captain Eworl was supposed to emerge from the elevator. Roger listened closely. Indeed, I would say he was rapt with attention. When I was finished, he remained still for a long time, thinking.

"You know you can't have Sarteen lose," he said finally. "It will wreck the story."

"She's not about to lose. She's preparing to die so that she can save the rest of her people."

Roger shook his head. "That's no good. You have to figure out a way for her to survive, too."

"She can only survive by surrendering. She won't do that. It's against her nature."

"You're the writer. You can adapt her nature any way you chose. Besides, you're missing my point.

You can't have a downer ending. People don't like them. It won't sell."

"Not everything I write has to sell. The story can have meaning in and of itself."

"Couldn't Sarteen fake surrender? Give in for the time being? Plan for a future revenge?"

"I don't think so. Once the Orions get their hands on you, I think you're pretty much their property. Sarteen would rather die first."

"You can't have her be a failure."

I had to smile. "Who's the writer here? Who's the actor?"

He nodded. "I wouldn't mind being in a movie made from this story. I could play Captain Eworl."

"So far he's only a voice across black space. He hasn't even been on stage."

"You said it yourself, the story isn't complete." Roger nodded. "Before it's over, I think he'll have a significant role."

The property Henry had chosen to build our "shark set" on was in the valley, actually in the foothills of the San Bernardino Mountains. The two hundred acres was a mismatch of hard orange soil and lovely pine and spruce trees. It was entirely fenced in—twenty-foot-high barriers topped with barbed wire. Even so, for insurance reasons, we had been required by law to have a security guard on the premises at all times. Couldn't have little boys and girls who lived in the vicinity digging under the fence and going for a swim with the sharks. Such a thing wouldn't enhance my newborn production company's reputation. I had personally hired the night security guard and he was only too happy to let us on the property. Yet he said he hadn't seen Bob. Roger shook his head at the comment.

"I told you so," he said. "He's home, sleeping. A guy that fat needs his rest."

"He told me he'd meet me at the boat. We've come this far. We may as well check it out."

Because of the bumps in the path, we couldn't drive the Corvette to the boat and manmade lake, although I would have preferred driving. The set was located at the far end of the property; it was a good quarter-mile walk from the entrance, a long hike in the middle of the night without a flashlight. If Bob was on the set, he had come in via an unknown back way. Roger took my hand as we walked. It wasn't easy to pull away from him. Light from the waning moon aided us, although I did stumble several times. But each time Roger was there to catch me.

"He said this situation was all set up by nature, and by ourselves. That we test ourselves."

I wondered what the yogi had meant.

We found Bob standing in the center of the boat, which was tied to the shore, his back to us. Moving closer, I noted the fins of the sharks as the maneaters circulated in the oval pond, viscous silver knives in the glow of the moon. Henry had rented four sharks. With the right angles and editing, he said, we could make it look like a whole school. Four were enough for my tastes. Andy's boyfriend had completed the backdrop. The fake daytime Caribbean sky, dimmed by the night, pressed in on us from three separate angles. Bob must have heard us approaching but he didn't turn until we actually stepped aboard the boat.

He had a gun in his hand.

"Bob," I said, stunned. "What the hell?"

He flashed the fiendish grin that worked so well on the screen. That made you believe that, yes, here was a young man capable of stranding kids aboard a sinking sailboat in the middle of shark-infested waters. At that moment he looked exactly as I had created Bob, before I even met him. Bob *was* Bob.

"Hello, Shari," he said. "Hello, Roger. Nice of you both to come. Please don't shout out or I'll have to shoot you."

"What do you want?" Roger asked.

Bob shook his gun a bit. "Oh, I'd think what I want is obvious. I want to rehearse."

"Huh?" I said.

Bob laughed bitterly. "You think you have such a great imagination, Ms. Best-selling Shari Cooper. You plot your stories so carefully. You sit at your computer and develop the motivation for your characters. What they were like as children. What they suffered as they went to school. Why they became criminals when they grew older. But you know nothing! Real criminals don't need motivation at all. We want to kill someone, we kill them. It's as simple as that."

Roger took a step forward. "Give me that gun, punk."

Bob raised the gun sharply, pointing it at Roger's face. "I will give you what's inside the gun before I hand it over. Understand me, Pretty Boy?"

Roger paused, chewed on that for a few seconds. "You say you want to rehearse. What scene?"

Bob nodded in admiration. "Pretty Boy is pretty smart. Yeah, the three of us are going to rehearse *First to Die's* climactic scene. Shari's going to take the lifeboat here, and ride it to the far side of the pond, then return for you to do it. If you both make it, you both live. Easy, huh? Of course, if she makes it that far, she can always run for safety. Hide in the trees. The idea might occur to her, and she might get away from me. I'm not in the best shape. On the other hand, she might not escape. I do have a gun. There aren't many places to hide here. Besides, if she does choose to flee, I get to push you in the water, Pretty Boy. Then you get to swim to the far side of the pond. Get out on this side and I shoot you."

"You're insane," Roger swore.

"Perhaps. I'm also creative. I'm a budding director. To add drama to the scene, before you guys appeared, I dropped a handful of bloody meat in the pond. Not enough to satisfy the sharks' hunger, you understand, but enough to get them thinking about their next meal. You can see how restlessly they're circling. They know good things are coming their way."

I moved to Roger's side, feeling oddly removed from the scene, as if this couldn't be happening to me. But my disinterest was rooted in shock and gave me no comfort. Bob was deadly serious. He was my own nightmare come to life. With his small revolver, he motioned me toward the small rubber lifeboat.

"There's no point in waiting," he said.

I had to struggle to draw a breath, to speak. "There's something wrong with this lifeboat."

Bob acted surprised. "Really? Is that possible? The union boys went over it this afternoon, just to be sure it was safe. It couldn't have a hole in it. Not unless it developed one recently. But maybe you're right, and the raft does have a small hole leaking air. Maybe that's another plot twist. You're the writer, Shari, you tell me. Could it be that the longer you delay taking the lifeboat, the more air runs out of it?"

"Does the motor work?" I asked.

Bob shrugged. "Can't tell you. You might take the time to check it out. Or you might just get your ass in gear and paddle to the other side of the pond and back."

I moved toward the lifeboat. Roger grabbed my arm. "Don't," he said. "It's a setup. You'll die."

I shook him off. "I'd rather the sharks got me than him."

Roger caught my eye. "Be careful."

Bob laughed. "How romantic! Be careful! What clever dialogue! God, if you don't need a regular doctor in a few minutes, you certainly need a script doctor."

"I should never have hired you," I muttered under my breath as I leaned over and studied the lifeboat floating off the port side. Bob, at least, had gone to the trouble to put it in the water for me. The problem was, in the poor light, I was unable to judge how much air it had lost. I wouldn't know until I jumped into it. Then, if it sank, it would probably be the last thing I knew. "Jesus," I whispered.

What would it feel like to have a hand bitten off? A foot? My blood would squirt into the water in a warm red stream. The only thing that would stop it would be another, larger bite, one that ripped off an entire limb, and forced my heart to stop beating. That's all the victim of a multiple shark attack could pray for, a quick end. For the second time since I had returned to Earth as a Wanderer, I could not believe the Rishi could have allowed me to fall into such a terrible predicament.

"But can't you protect me?"

"Protect you from what? Death? There is no death. I have nothing to protect you from."

That was easy to say when you didn't have a physical body to worry about.

"Shari," Roger said behind me.

"I can do it," I said tightly. Summoning my courage, I crouched down and planted my left arm on the sailboat deck. Spinning through a half hop, I swung my legs over and into the lifeboat. It didn't sink, but wobbled badly. The sharks sensed the movement and swam closer. Glancing up, I saw Roger creep to the edge and peer down at me. Bob stood behind him, the pistol to Roger's head.

"Since you performed that move so gracefully," Bob said, "I will give you a helpful hint. There's no gas in the motor." He gestured to the far side of the pond. "Better hurry, Shari. A sinking raft always takes longer to paddle back."

There was one paddle in the lifeboat, not two. Picking it up, I scooted to the center of the raft and began to paddle frantically. Naturally I began to swing in circles. On the deck of the sailboat set, Bob hooted.

"She's playing with the sharks! She thinks they're really dolphins!"

"Shut up," I muttered. The key to successful paddling must be not to freak out. Stabilizing the raft by paddling first on one side, then on the other, I steadily began to plow toward the far shore, increasing my speed as I gained confidence. In reality, the pond was only forty yards across, less than half the length of a football field. It took me only a minute to traverse it. Behind me, I heard Roger call out.

"Run!" he cried. "He's playing with us! It's like your book! He'll kill us anyway."

In my heart I knew Roger was right. Bob couldn't possibly allow us to live if he planned to stay out of jail for the next forty years. Unfortunately, I couldn't leave Roger to such a gruesome death. Yet I lacked the ingenuity of the hero in my book. The raft was low on air, the sides were getting squishier.

Bob intended for Roger to paddle across and back next. A second of delay could make all the difference for him. Yet, in the end, it would probably make no difference at all. Bob would keep making us take turns until one of us went under and was turned into shark food.

Master! Help me! I promise to be good.

No brilliant insight came to me. Good was not good enough.

I paddled the lifeboat back to the sailboat.

Several feet above my head, Bob saluted my nobility by clapping.

"She thought about fleeing," he said. "But in the end true love won out over fear." He turned to Roger. "Your turn, Pretty Boy. Let's see what you're made of. The conditions are the same as before. If you flee, she goes in the water."

Roger glanced at the waning moon, seemed to think for a moment, then turned and straightened in Bob's direction. "No," he said firmly.

"Roger," I gasped.

Bob chuckled. "No? You say no to the Bad Boy with the big gun?" He cocked the hammer on the gun. "Not a smart move, Pretty Boy."

"I don't believe you have the guts to shoot me in cold blood," Roger said, staring him hard in the eye. His words were powerful—Bob actually took a step back, and for a moment seemed uncertain.

"What do you mean?" Bob asked.

Roger took a step toward him. "I mean you won't

195

shoot me. You're too fat, too slow, too stupid to destroy me. Isn't that so?"

Bob smiled quickly. "Yeah, that's it. I'm nothing next to you. Are you going in the raft or not?"

"No. You're going in the water."

"What?"

Roger lashed out with his right foot. He could have had a black belt in karate, his blow was that swift, that accurate. Suddenly the gun was not in Bob's hand. Bob was in Roger's hands. Wearing an expression of absolute terror, Bob was dangling over the edge of the sailboat, held only by Roger's vicelike grip.

"Time to meet the Grim Reaper," Roger said coldly.

"Wait!" Bob cried. "Don't! The sharks! They— Eeehh!"

Roger threw him overboard, over me. Bob's left foot caught my right cheek before he bellyflopped into the dark pond. Before he could resurface, the fins converged. Four silver arrows aimed at one thrashing late supper. Just prior to closing my eyes and ears to the screams, Bob managed to get his head above the water. His expression was as much bewildered as terror stricken. He started to say something to me, but water rolled into his mouth and he choked. Before he could recover, he jerked down slightly, a couple of times in a row. The jerks were not because of his own wild flailing, but were being applied externally. His face was as white as the pale moonlight that shone on him from high above. Yet, from far below, a dark liquid began to spread out from his struggling form. A warm, sticky fluid that would have been bright red had it been midday, but which, this many hours after midnight, was as black as an oil gusher.

The sharks had begun to feed.

I screamed as Bob screamed.

It seemed as if they fed a long time.

CHAPTER
XVII

*T*HE NEXT TWELVE HOURS were a blur for me. Roger ran for the guard, who called for the police. Twenty minutes later, five black and white units and two ambulances braved the bumps and drove up to the set. Their flashing lights spread hideous color over Bob's remains; the pieces of flesh bobbed like torn apples at a disastrous Halloween party. On a boulder fifty feet from the pond, I sat with my eyes closed and tried to block out the universe.

A death, especially one as bizarre as Bob's, was not something the LAPD brushed over without exhaustive hours of questioning and requestioning. Roger and I were separated and taken down to the station. Obviously the authorities wanted to see if our stories matched. It was only after five hours of questioning that I wondered if I should have freely waived my right to remain silent. What I was telling them sounded like a Shari Cooper novel! Trying to explain that what Bob had done was based on a novel of mine didn't help. The odd thing was, in the midst of it all, I never knew if I was under arrest. And here I was a mystery writer. Research had not prepared me for reality. Aliens were predictable next to people; they just wanted to conquer the Earth.

What had Bob wanted? I wondered that as the sun came up outside and my head throbbed with pain and fatigue. My questioning cops would not allow me a Tylenol-3, even though it was prescription medicine and I begged them for just one. They wanted me sharp. No drugged excuses for a defense attorney to drag up later in court. To put it simply, the men didn't believe me.

Poor Roger, I thought. He was the one who had thrown Bob in the water. I wondered how he was doing. Foolishly, I asked if I could see him. They shook their heads. Right then I would have stood a better chance of obtaining an audience with the Pope. I needed to have my confession heard. Even though, technically, I had done nothing wrong, I was plagued with guilt. The detectives must have sensed that and because of it didn't let me go or even rest. They hoped I would crack, spill my guts, sort of like the way Bob's had been spilled.

Finally I lost it. Pacing, I demanded that they at least give me a chance to place one call. I ranted about lawsuits and how they had no right to hold me and how I was a famous writer. A *New York Times* best-selling author, I yelled! That did it; that best-seller list always pushed the right buttons. They exchanged worried glances and shoved a phone in my direction. But who do you call at a time of crisis? Your family? Your lover? I felt as if I had already lost both. My producer was supposed to manage everything that happened on the set. I called Henry.

He was beautiful. He was down at the station within an hour with a high-priced lawyer who made the detectives scowl and go for doughnuts. Within the hour, I walked out of the station a free woman. The press was waiting for me, not at the back door—but at the front. Henry said the story had already hit the airways. The media even had a slogan ready. "Bob was first to die. Who will be next?" Henry promised he would get Roger out next. He drove me back to my hotel and there, after swallowing three of my pain pills, I collapsed on my bed and tried not to think, to even exist.

Yet, this time, I did dream.

If it was that, and not a vision.

I floated through outer space, the leader of a group of golden entities that needed no vessel to traverse vast distances. Up ahead, a blue-white globe shimmered in the endless river of stars, a living planet of inexpressible potential. This world was my destination. And although I was a creature of spirit and not of flesh and blood, I felt as if I might weep when I saw it again. Too long, I thought, to be isolated from Mother Earth. It didn't look so different from the last time I had seen it. Yet I knew much had changed since then. Much had died. The quarantine was to blame.

But that was why my partners and I had returned. To break it.

To plug the two strands of humanity's DNA back into the natural twelve.

To reconnect humanity to eternity.

Yet it took almost an eternity of time to accomplish the simplest task. I entered one body, lived a productive life. Tried to help where I could, to speak truth where superstition prevailed. To offer love where hate dominated. Then I died and had to start all over. Another body, another set of parents, of genes, of characteristics that make up a human personality. Around and around I traveled the wheel of reincarnation. Yet each time, between each birth and death, I was allowed a chance to pause, to rest and gather my strength, to see that not all our efforts were in vain. Despite the continuing dominance of the enemy, humanity slowly evolved over the centuries. Discarding the illusions of fear, of separateness, of not trusting in the divine plan. Of having no faith in their own immortality. It was to increase this faith that I fought the hardest. For it constituted the enemy's greatest hold on humanity. Without the fear of death and the dogma of judgmental religions and brain-washing cults that grew up around them, the quarantine would have crumbled in the twinkling of a distant star. So again I returned to life to shout out that there was only life and no end to our being. No devil could claim our souls for all eternity unless we created the devil ourselves. Some heard me; most did not. It didn't matter. In my soul I knew that in the end, we would be triumphant.

Yet, occasionally, even I stumbled. The enemy fooled me. And those were not lives I remembered with joy. Indeed, sometimes, in my desire to make my mark on the world, I made the mistake of doing the enemy's work.

When I opened my eyes it was almost dark. Immediately I sat up and turned on the light. I had slept away the entire day. If my dream were true—and I could only recall fragments of it—then I had also slept away the last few years. Had the Rishi ever told me that I was special? I assumed he had. Since my rebirth, I had taken pride in the fact that I was a Wanderer. A best-selling writer who could save humanity with my amazing stories. Right—I couldn't even save myself. Yet the Rishi had said many things that emphasized the specialness of each of us.

"Those of negative vibration crave power and dominance. That is their trademark. You can spot them that way. They try to place themselves above others. They feel they are especially chosen by God for a great purpose. But God chooses everyone and all his purposes are great."

The yogi had said similar words.

"That is a form of enlightenment. To feel like everyone belongs to you, and you belong to them. That is something a Master will always teach. There is no hierarchy in the family of man. We are all equal, all children of the divine. The Master is the

same as the student, the disciple, the devotee. The Master never places himself above them because if he did then he wouldn't be able to help them. That's why we don't seek power. Those things separate us from each other. They lead to ignorance, to darkness."

Why hadn't I been able to see that it was the Rishi who spoke to me through the body of the yogi? That their truth was one? I had wanted proof, a miracle. Even after the yogi had given me the miracle of my own inner peace, I left him. And for what? To make out with Roger? What had my choice brought me but misery?

Reaching over, I picked up the phone and called Peter.

Jacob answered.

"Hello?"

"Jacob, this is Shari. How are you?"

He hesitated. "I'm OK, but we want you to come home. Peter misses you. I miss you."

I forced a laugh. "I'll come home, tonight. I promise. Is Peter there?"

"No. He's with the yogi."

"The yogi is still in town? I thought he was leaving."

"He is tonight. He's giving a talk at a house in Orange County now."

"Do you know where the house is? The address?"

"No."

"Did Peter happen to write down the address on a scrap of paper? Is there one lying around?"

"I can't see one."

"Oh God, I'm sorry, Jacob. That was stupid of me to say."

"There probably is a scrap of paper here that has directions on it. I know Peter was talking to the people at the house just before he left."

I paused. "Did Peter call these people for directions?"

"Yes."

"Have you made any calls since then?"

"No. I wouldn't use your phone without permission. I couldn't use this one if I wanted to. The buttons are different than the ones on other phones. I don't know what to push."

"Jacob, listen very carefully. The button on the lower right-hand side is the Redial button. Don't push it now, but when I hang up I want you to push it. It will almost certainly dial the number of the house where Peter and the yogi are. Whoever answers, tell that person it is crucial for Peter Jacobs to call me immediately at the Beverly Hills Hotel. Can you remember that?"

"Yes. I have a good memory. I will get him for you and have him call you. I know he wants to talk to you a whole bunch."

"I want to talk to him a whole bunch. Hey, when's your next game?"

"Tomorrow. Can you come?"

"You bet. I'll be there."

"Can we go to Disneyland again?"

"Yes. Tomorrow." I don't know why there were

tears in my eyes. "We can do everything tomorrow, Jacob."

We exchanged goodbyes. A few minutes later the phone rang. It wasn't Peter but a woman at the house where the yogi was staying. Peter, she said, was in a private meeting with the yogi. But she would be happy to give me her address, which was what I wanted most. She told me to be sure to hurry, the yogi's plane was to leave in two hours.

"Tell him I'm coming," I cried.

"What's your name?" she asked.

"He knows my name."

CHAPTER

XVIII

*B*UT I HAD PUT OFF seeing the yogi one time too many. When I reached the house, he had gone. Peter waited outside in front for me, in his wheel-chair, a red rose resting in his lap. When he told me the news, I was devastated.

"But I need to talk to him," I cried. "Can we go to the airport?"

Peter shook his head. "He leaves from LAX, on the other side of town. He left here a while ago. By the time we got there he would probably be board-ing." He handed me the rose. "He told me to give you this."

I smelled it—such a lovely fragrance. "Did he say anything else about me?"

"Yes. He said to tell you, 'The writer has many stories in her. Whenever one comes to an end, another begins.'" Peter paused, then added, "He also told me to say that you have nothing to fear, that all has been taken care of."

"What did he mean?"

"I don't know. He acted like you'd know what he meant."

I was puzzled. Every word of his meant so much. It was difficult to know where to apply his advice to my life. But perhaps it had yet to be applied. Leaning over, I gave Peter a big hug.

"I missed you, my love," I whispered in his ear. "Do you still want me back?"

He had tears in his eyes. "Yes. Will you come back?"

"Yes." I kissed him. "And I will never leave you. Never ever."

"What made up your mind?"

I straightened up, glancing up and down the street. The strangest sensation flowed through me. It was as if I were being filmed, studied, dissected. Yet no one was there. A shiver made its way through my body as I thought of Bob, what was left of him.

"Something happened last night," I said. "It was terrible. Then something beautiful happened this afternoon while I slept."

"While you were asleep?"

"Yes. I had a dream. It explained so much to me. It put me in my place, so to speak, and also reminded me of several important things the Rishi and the yogi both said. Plus it helped me remember other dreams I've been having lately, and what they mean." I shrugged. "I know I'm speaking like a crazy woman again. But what's important is that I feel clearer now. I won't be seeing Roger anymore."

Peter was grateful. "Good." He paused. "What are you looking for?"

I shrugged, although I continued to feel watched. "Nothing."

"What happened last night?"

"It's a long story. Can I tell you later? At home?"

"Yes," he said. "Do you want to go there now?"

"Yes. It's a shame we came in separate cars. We can't drive together." I kissed him again. "I don't want to leave you for a minute!"

He patted my side. "We'll live happily ever after," he promised. "Like in the movies."

I laughed. "Like in a book, silly. Books are better."

Peter followed me in his van, as was our custom. I always fought my way to the front to be the leader. To be important. That would stop now, I vowed. I would live as the yogi had said: simply, naturally, like grass.

Stopped at a light, I picked up my car phone and checked my messages. There were several from Garrett. His tone was urgent, I dialed him immediately. He answered on the first ring.

"This is Garrett."

"This is Jean Rodrigues. I'm sorry about missing our appointment. I was tied up."

"I heard about why you were tied up. Roger Teller was with you when the young man died?"

"Yes. Bob tried to kill Roger and me."

"Really?" Garrett said sarcastically.

"You sound doubtful. I was there, I know what happened."

"You sound doubtful yourself. It doesn't matter. I have to meet with you tonight."

"You found out something about Roger?"

There was an odd note in his voice. "Yes. Among other things."

"I see," I replied, although I didn't really. "Where would you like to meet?"

"Where are you now?"

"In my car, in Newport Beach."

"That's perfect. I'm in Orange County as well. Let's meet at the entrance to the Huntington Beach Pier."

My old stomping ground. "Why there?"

That odd tone again. "Is there something wrong with it?"

"No. I can come. I'll be there in twenty minutes."

"I'll be waiting," Garrett said as he hung up.

Peter had a car phone as well, a necessity because of his handicap. I called him, and after explaining that I had to meet with Garrett about Roger, I told him to go on home and take care of Jacob. I'd catch up with him soon. But Peter insisted on accompanying me. I believe he was curious to see Garrett. Together, we drove to Huntington Beach Pier, which was only two miles south of where I had died as Shari Cooper.

"Why there?"

Garrett had sounded like he had a lot on his mind.

He was standing at the pier entrance as we arrived. We just pulled over to the side of the road, staying on the Coast Highway. Garrett walked over to my Jag, and I rolled down the window. He nodded to the van behind me.

"Who's your friend?" he asked.

"My boyfriend." I looked around. "Do you want us to park and maybe talk in a coffee shop or something?"

"No, and I don't want to talk here. Can I just get in?"

I hesitated. "Sure. You want to go somewhere else?"

"Yes," he said. "It's not far."

"Fine. Get in."

As Garrett climbed into the passenger seat, I called Peter and told him to follow us. Everything was cool. But maybe *cool* was the wrong word. Garrett, as he glanced over at me, looked like he had just seen a ghost. Or *was* seeing a ghost. His skin was pale with a sheen of fine perspiration, yet his eyes were as sharp as ever.

"Where do you want to go?" I asked.

"Don't you know?"

Damn! "No."

He noticed my discomfort. "It's just down the road a bit."

"What is?"

"A certain condominium. You're sure you're not familiar with it?"

"I don't know what you're talking about."

"Would you have any objection to going to this

condo? I've already been there this afternoon. It's unoccupied—a bunch of empty rooms. Even the carpet's gone. The manager, Rita Wilde, said I could drop by it whenever I wished." He paused. "Do you know Rita?"

"No," I lied.

He nodded to himself as he studied my reaction. "I know her from a few years back. I met her when I was investigating a death at the condo."

I shuddered. "We don't have to go there."

"But I want to. I think it's the right place to talk." He reached over and put his hand on my arm. "What do you think?"

My voice was shaky. "I told you what I think."

"Are you afraid?"

"No."

"Are you concerned that the place might be haunted?"

"No."

"Then let's go. We're blocking traffic. It's only two miles north of here."

"OK." I put my Jag in gear.

Peter must have known our destination because he fell back a bit as if he didn't want to follow. Yet he did not drive away. Garret was, of course, right. For me the condo was as haunted as a cemetery. I hadn't been back to it since the day I reaquainted myself with Jimmy. With my badly disguised uneasiness, I wasn't fooling Garrett one bit. Clearly he had read *Remember Me;* nevertheless, I decided to let him wonder and admit to nothing. The whole way there, I forced him to give me directions.

We parked outside the condo, I believe, exactly where my friends and I had parked the night I died. Peter rolled out the van's side door in his wheelchair as we walked over to him. He wasn't happy about our meeting place.

"Why are we here?" he demanded.

"Garrett wants to talk to us here," I said. "Detective Garrett, this is my boyfriend—Lenny. Lenny, meet Garrett."

Garrett shook Peter's hand. "How did you two meet?" he asked.

"It's a long story," I muttered.

He gave me a knowing look. "I'm sure it is."

We went upstairs, took the elevator. To the fourth floor. When you fall off a fourth floor—if you're into such things, which I don't recommend—the police speak of your falling *three* stories to your death. Because you fall only three stories since you begin such a plunge from the *floor* of the fourth floor. The details don't really matter. If you land on your head on concrete—as I had—you die.

Garrett led us to what had once been the Palmone residence.

The door was unlocked. We went inside. Turned on the lights. It was dark now.

A cool ocean breeze blew in from the open balcony door.

I tried but couldn't stop trembling.

I ran from the room then, through the kitchen and out onto the balcony and into the night. I remember standing by the rail, feeling the smooth wood beneath my shaking fingers. I remember seeing the flat black ocean and thinking how nice it would be if I could only exercise my magical powers and fly over to it and disappear beneath its surface for ages to come. I remember time passing.

Then things went bad.

"Are you cold?" Garrett asked.

I lowered my head. "Yes," I whispered.

"Have you been here before?" he asked.

I shook my head.

"Did you know that someone died here?"

"You just told me."

"Shari Cooper died here. Did you know her?"

"No."

"Why did you choose that name for your pen name?"

His gaze was steady and bored into me, but his will wavered. He didn't really want the truth from me. When all was said and done, the truth was terrifying. Especially when we needed to hang on to our limited ideas of selves and the universe. Truly, as the Rishi had said, modern religion's attempt to define with words the ultimate reality was the ultimate blasphemy. Garrett looked at me as if he couldn't decide to swear at me or plead with me.

"It's just a name," I said. "It means nothing."

Garrett shook his head. "I read your book."

I sighed. "Did you enjoy it?"

"How could you write that book? How could you know those things? You put me in your book!"

"I had never met you until two days ago."

"You put my daughter in your book!" He took a step toward me, roughly grabbed my shoulder.

"She went into hysterics when she read your epilogue!"

Peter started to intervene but I motioned him to stay back. I continued to hold Garrett's eyes, trying to tell him silently that these were questions better left unasked and unanswered. For his own sanity. Yet I was the one who had decided the story should be published. I was as responsible for his daughter's confusion as I was responsible for her recovery from drug addiction.

"I'm sorry I upset your daughter," I said. "I realize my book upset a lot of people. But it will help even more people. It's an important story. I had to tell it. But it's just a story. Think of it that way. For you, I believe, that would be best." I paused. "We don't need to stay here. Whatever happened here, it's in the past. We should go."

Garrett released me and turned away, his shoulders sagging. He could have aged fifteen years since I walked into his office three days ago. It was as if I had stabbed him with my revelations of how he had solved the mystery of my death, stabbed him with a blade that had created deeper mysteries. The condo was cool but he was now drenched with sweat.

"You're not going to tell me anything?" he said, his back to me.

"It's just a story," I repeated.

"But the things you described. No one could . . ." He whirled as if to pounce on me with another barrage of questions. Then the strength seemed to flow out of him. He glanced around the empty rooms, shaking his head. He spoke in a soft, weary voice. "That night, after I finished questioning the kids, I sat here and drank scotch and tried to figure out what had really happened. I drew a sketch of the condo layout. I paced through the rooms several times and drew an X where I believed the murderer—if there had been a murderer—must have stood when he or she pushed Shari Cooper to her death. Then I found an orange stain on the floor. Clay that matched the tiles on the roof. It was a fresh stain, not the sort of thing you would leave on your floor if you were about to invite people over for a birthday party. It was then I knew someone at the party had been up on the roof. It was then I knew that Shari had probably been killed."

"That soon?" I asked despite myself.

He nodded. "Yes. I knew at the beginning. But what I didn't know was—" He paused.

"What?" I asked.

"That Shari Cooper was watching me that night. That the whole time I drank and worked to figure out who had killed her, she was pacing nearby. That she was there, trying to help me. It's an amazing thought." He rubbed his head and groaned. "If you think about it, it could drive you crazy."

"I'm sure she'd have liked to help you," I said gently.

He nodded and briefly closed his eyes. When he opened them, his expression was softer. He didn't want to interrogate me; he just wanted peace of mind. Even before he asked his last question, I knew I had to try to give him that peace. I owed him so much.

"Do you know if Shari and Peter did finally enter the light?" he asked.

I glanced at Peter and smiled at Garrett. "Yes. They made it into the light. It waits for all of us. In this world or the next."

He nodded faintly. "Thank you."

"Thank you," I said. "From both of us."

Garrett let my comment sink in, then suddenly glanced at Peter, then nodded again to himself. He was a good man, a smart man. I believe he understood much more than I said aloud. After a moment he shook himself as if emerging from a dream.

"I have to tell you about Roger Teller," he said. "He's a bad seed. Much worse than either of us imagined."

I raised my hand. "Not here. This is not a good place to talk about such things." I turned for the door. "Let's get out of here."

But before we could move the lights went out.

The darkness was absolute. I couldn't see the others.

Then the lights clicked on. Roger stood just inside the doorway.

The gun he carried looked like Bob's.

Bob, I understood at that moment, had not intended to harm us.

In that awful moment I understood many mysterious things.

"Am I a bad seed?" Roger asked Garrett. "I've never been described that way before." He motioned to all of us. "Out on the balcony."

I stood firm. "It's me you want. Let the others go."

Roger chuckled. "I can have you that much better with the others out of the way." He shook his gun again. "I'm an impatient individual."

And he didn't want to be kept waiting. We went out onto the balcony. The cool breeze continued to blow. The ocean was not a flat black lagoon as it had been the night I died, but rough—a sorcerer's dark pot of boiling brew. Three stories below I saw the lamppost, which had rushed toward me during my fatal plunge. I also saw the faint outline of my bloodstain. Rita Wilde said the mark refused to wash away completely.

"What do you want?" Garrett demanded.

Roger motioned to the railing. "Sit up there."

"You're insane," Garrett swore.

Roger raised his gun and pointed it at Garrett's face. He cocked the hammer, and put enough pressure on the trigger that a single sneeze would fire the gun, and Garrett would have a hole in his head.

"Do as I say," Roger said coldly.

Garrett sat on the railing. Peter and I waited. But what we waited for, I didn't know. God may have worked in mysterious ways, but he didn't work as well when the other guy had the gun. Yet I prayed to him all the same, and to the Rishi and the yogi.

Garrett is a wonderful man! The world needs his wonder!

Roger put the gun to Garrett's forehead. "Tell me," he said. "What kind of crop does a bad seed bring?"

Garrett was fearless. "The usual scum like you."

Roger grinned. "I don't like your answer."

Garrett snorted. "Go to hell."

Roger lost his grin. "I may go there. But not today."

Roger shoved Garrett hard in the chest. The man went over the side.

Like me, he didn't scream. Like me, he landed hard, and on his head.

His skull cracked. Blood splattered everywhere.

Such a gruesome sight—no human should have to behold it.

My eyes closed. God closed both our eyes. Garrett died instantly.

"It waits for all of us. In this world or the next."

"I know," I whispered. "The light will wait for a man such as you."

A hand roughly grabbed my arm.

"Come," Roger said. "The night's young. We have somewhere special to go."

CHAPTER

XIX

*H*E TOOK US TO the cemetery where I was buried. I knew he would. He had a flair for the dramatic, and he was a sick person. It was getting on toward eleven o'clock. The cemetery was a large, lonely field of rolling blackness. As he goaded us toward my grave, I was surprised to see that he had already visited the spot earlier. The gravesite had been uncovered, not an easy task, what with concrete liners and other stuff grave diggers used nowadays. My tombstone lay toppled nearby. A shovel rested on top of the mound of brown dirt. Roger had probably worked up a sweat digging it all out. I remarked on the fact and he shoved his gun deeper into my spine, causing me to bump into Peter's wheelchair, which I helped wheel over the uneven ground.

"Shut up and keep moving," he said.

"Talk about bad dialogue," I said. "You were going to edit my script? You couldn't edit the ingredients on a can of dog food."

"Your mouth is going to be the death of you."

"Then I may as well talk while I can. You've been following me."

"For longer than you know, sister."

"How did you set Bob up?"

"Easy. He wanted to play a prank on you. I showed him how. Getting into the secured area was easy; he just dug a hole and went under the fence. He was going to let us go after I returned in the lifeboat. We just took a little air out of the tubes. There was no hole. There was never any real danger from the sharks."

"For you and me," I said.

"For me," he corrected. "I almost put you in the pond last night."

"Why didn't you? Death by shark bite—you can't get much better than that."

"Just wait," he promised.

"Who are you?" I asked. "Or should I say, *what* are you?"

"I'm surprised you haven't figured that out."

"Just as many Wanderers are incarnating on Earth to help with the transition, many with negative vibrations are also returning to stop it. They will not succeed, but they can upset the plans of many men and women of good will. In particular, they dislike Wanderers and attack them when they have the chance."

"You're a Black Wanderer. You're an Orion. You're a lousy kisser."

He smacked me on the back of my head with his gun. "Shut up!"

"You're an out-of-work actor," Peter said, putting in his own two cents' worth.

Roger was bitter. "I don't need your money or your starring roles. Our kind are well financed. We have structure. We obey orders. Your friend's detective friend in Chicago will discover that the hard way tomorrow. He will pay for snooping into our business."

"How old were you when you realized what you were?" I asked curiously.

"I have always known I had a great destiny."

I stopped thirty feet short of my grave and turned around, knowing he might shoot me, but not really giving a damn. I was so pissed at him. The hatred drowned out my fear. Yet I doubted it would hold the fear at bay when the mud began to fill my lungs. That he intended to bury me alive was a given.

"Why did you come after me?" I asked. "What was I doing that was so disturbing?"

Surprisingly, he acted pleased to tell me the truth. "You know the answer to that. You were beginning to write books that broke down established concepts. We couldn't have that. Those concepts are the keys to control. Control is the secret of power. We especially couldn't allow you to publish your story of the invasion and the establishment of the quarantine. People might not consciously understand it, but it could stir ancient memories."

What he said shocked me, and I had written the story. The whole situation was madness. From the outside he was just a cute guy. Except he was pointing a gun at me.

"My story took place in the future," I protested.

Roger shook his head. "In the past. Three hundred thousand years ago."

"But in my story humanity had starships. We traveled the galaxy."

"And so your people did. Until we stopped them and put them in their place."

"Wow," I mumbled, astonished I had such a heavy muse working for me. Then my pride resurfaced. "You didn't stop all of us. I know now what Sarteen did. She exploded that egg. She wasn't afraid to sacrifice her life. I see the moral of the tale, why I wrote it. Others will as well. It is better to die free of the lies of the quarantine than to live beneath the tyranny of its illusions. Sarteen defeated your precious Captain Eworl. Not all of humanity was trapped."

Roger was haughty. "So what? The few of you who come here accomplish nothing. We find you and we kill you. Look at your supposedly great leaders. They never last long."

"Yeah, but we keep coming. We don't give up. And I think we've got you by the throat now. A new era is rolling in. Your fire-and-brimstone fear tactics don't work anymore. People don't buy the devil chasing their souls. They're coming back to what's inside. They're listening to what the yogi and others like him are teaching."

Roger snorted. "Him? He's just another ignored prophet."

"I didn't ignore him. Yeah, maybe for a short time I fell for your charm. But in my heart I was always with him, and he with me. He's with Peter and me now. Go ahead and put us in the ground. You won't see either of us beg for mercy. We know you have no mercy. We've died before and know that death doesn't exist. It's just another lie you propagate on the ignorant." I spat in his face. "I'm glad I never had sex with you. That's one thing I have to be proud of. The snake never got to me."

He slapped me in the face with his gun. A numbing pain spread through both my cheeks and a wave of dizziness swept over me. Sticky blood dripped from my nose. I believed he'd broken it. This time I had pushed him too far. Yet it was interesting what his anger revealed, and what my choice of words indicated. Ancient memories were indeed being stirred. For a moment his features blurred and elongated. I blinked and thought I saw a toothy maw, a wide snout, and knew it was a vision similar to what Sarteen had beheld when the elevator door aboard her starship had opened. In fact, for all I knew, I had been Sarteen.

And Roger, he was a lizard.

"You *will* scream before I'm through with you," he promised.

I laughed. "You sound like Bob in my book."

He threw me into the grave on top of my black coffin with its gold trim, which had faded. I landed on my back, smashing my skull on the metal. The shock brought another wave of dizziness. Red stars, the color and consistency of fireworks, danced

223

across my field of vision. Peter, strangely silent, was forced to sit at the edge of the hole and watch it all. Roger picked up his shovel and threw a few pounds of dirt in my face as I struggled to climb out. The force of the earth caused me to stumble and fall. While I lay momentarily helpless, another two shovelfuls landed on top of me. My resolve not to cry out weakened. Edgar Allan Poe had been right. There was no worse way to go than live burial.

"Peter." I coughed, trying to roll over and push myself up, to at least die standing on my feet. But such a position was not recommended in Roger Teller's *Book of Games & Graves.* I got as far as my knees when Roger swung his shovel through a wide curving arc and caught me on the right temple with the steel blade. The pain was intense, a thing of Biblical proportions. Smashing against the wall of the hole, I felt as if my scalp had been lifted three inches and a balloon filled with red liquid beneath it had popped. I lost a pint of blood in five seconds. It spread over the top of my coffin like the melting wax of a red candle. Worse, he had hit me precisely where I was weakest, where my headaches always started. The internal damage became very much external. It was a miracle I didn't lose consciousness or topple over. Yet it was not a miracle I would have prayed for to God. Better that my nightmare should end quickly, I thought. From out of the corner of my left eye, I watched Roger toss his shovel aside and crouch beside the hole, peering down at me with a grin so idiotic that if I hadn't been bleeding so much, I swear I would have vomited in his face.

"Now," Roger said pleasantly. "If you will just open the coffin and take out what's inside, I might stop throwing dirt on top of you. What do you say?"

I wiped at my face, trying to get one last look at Peter. In either body, he was my darling. I wanted to leave this life with him on my mind. I didn't imagine Roger would let him live long after I was gone.

Yet I couldn't find him.

He wasn't in his chair.

Roger continued to grin.

"Does that sound like a deal, Shari Ann Cooper?" he asked.

Then I saw Peter. He was standing!

"No," I replied.

Peter was bending over and picking up the shovel!

Roger leaned over to hear me better. "You said no? To me?"

Peter raised the shovel over his head.

I smiled through my blood. "Yes, Roger. I'm turning you down again."

Peter brought down the shovel hard on the back of Roger's head. Peter's aim was precise, driven by a supernatural will. The monster tumbled into the grave; he fell facedown onto the coffin. The back of his head was split open. His blood poured out and mingled with my mine, creating a puddle of ooze that looked as if it had been spilled from a victim of the black plague. A cursed puddle that spread as if pumped from within, even though Roger's dark eyes lay wide open and staring at a nothingness as hopeless as his long-range plans had been. He was dead.

"Thank God," I whispered.

Then I collapsed beside the enemy.

CHAPTER

XX

*T*HE ANSWER TO THE MYSTERY of Peter's healing lay in the yogi's words to him at the public lecture. *"It is this love that will heal you. Nothing ever heals except divine love. It is all that there is."* Peter later said that watching me be tortured to death was painful beyond belief. Yet it was that pain that forced him to act on a love that we, as mere mortals, have trouble believing exists, divine love. It was grace, truly, that allowed him to stand, to defeat the enemy. It was grace that allowed the change in his spinal cord to remain permanent. It is now five days after the attack and he walks fine. The karma of his past suicide has been burnt to ash.

But what about my karma? Peter took me to the hospital after the struggle at the cemetery. There I regained consciousness and allowed the doctors to sew my scalp together—forty prickling stitches. Yet I refused to stay for further tests, even though the pain in my head was unbearable. Intuitively, I understood there was nothing they could do for me.

Roger shattered the last threads of blood vessel that had kept Jean Rodrigues's brain functioning the past three years. There was not much time left. Knowing that, I went home to write this story, my last story.

It is dark in my apartment as I work. Peter and Jacob are asleep. Outside my window, I see the wide expanse of the black ocean, feel the cool salty breeze. It is a childish observation but it has always amazed me how the color of the sea changes with the color of the sky. Yet, in the same way, life also changes with the color of our emotions. Now, as I write these words, even though it is night, the world looks bright to me. At last, I am at peace.

I know how to finish "The Starlight Crystal."

At that moment the elevator door opened.
Sarteen saw Captain Eworl.
She *did* recognize him.

Just a second. Before I continue I have to jot down an old fable. Sarteen's grandmother told it to the future starship captain one night when the then five-year-old girl was about to go to bed. The story comes to me as I write, like an old memory.

There was once a dragon who lived in a wishing well. He had been there for many years, but always stayed out of sight, at the bottom in the pitch dark, where the water was cold as ice. When people visited the well, they never saw the dragon. Yet sometimes they heard him— his voice more like thoughts in their minds than whispers in their ears. Standing beside the well, people would be seized by the belief that if they wished for something, it would come true. But only if they wished hard and offered to give something in return. For that was the condition the dragon always made. He had the power to fulfill dreams, yet his price was high. Because people, not knowing that they were praying to a dragon, would sometimes say out loud, "I would give my right arm to be famous." Or, "I would give my health to live in such a wonderful house." Or, "I would give anything to find true love."

This last wish pleased the dragon the most because then he could take *everything* from that person, and give nothing in return. Because, of course, love is the one thing a dragon can never give. It is the one thing a dragon knows nothing about, and the person would die broken-hearted. Yet if the person wished for fame or a house, the dragon could easily dole that out, and then take the person's arm or health, whatever had been offered in return for the prize. The man would become well-known and then have an accident and his arm would be severed from his body. The woman would move into her new home and then have a nervous breakdown trying to take care of it. Always the dragon would get his reward, and always the person would suffer for having asked for anything.

But one day a young but wise girl came to the well. Knowing its reputation as a wish-giving well, she asked for happiness. The request was unusual; the dragon had never received it before. True, many people asked for certain things to make them happy, but no one asked for happiness itself. Curious to know this person better, the dragon crawled out of the well and showed the girl his true form. He was surprised that she didn't back away from him in horror. Indeed, his first question to her was "Why aren't you afraid of me?"

"Why should I be?" the girl asked.

"Because I'm a dragon. Everybody is afraid of me."

The girl laughed. "Well, I'm not. You don't scare me one bit. You just look like a big, ugly lizard to me. Do you really have magical powers?"

The dragon was offended. "Yes. My powers are well known."

"Then grant me my wish. Give me happiness."

"Not so fast. If I give you this, what will you give me in return?"

"My sorrow," the girl said simply.

The dragon laughed. "What kind of bargain is that? I don't want your sorrow. If I give you happiness, then you must give me something special in return."

"What do you want from me?"

The dragon thought. "How about your heart?"

The girl considered. "All right. You give me happiness, and in return I'll give you my heart. In fact, to show you what a good sport I am, I'll give you my heart first. But if afterward you fail to give me happiness, then you must give me your head. You must allow me to cut it off with a sword."

"What do you want with my head?"

"It's none of your business. I just want it."

The dragon was amused. He believed the girl was a fool. If I take her heart, he thought, she'll be dead. I'll have what I want and I won't have to give her anything in return. The dragon believed he was making the best bargain of his long life.

"Agreed," the dragon said. "I'll cut out your heart and then I'll give you happiness. If I fail to do so, you can cut off my head."

"Fine." The girl stepped close so that the dragon could reach her. Spreading out her arms, she said, "Take my heart, you ugly lizard."

The dragon reached over and clawed open the girl's chest and pulled out her heart. Immediately the girl fell to the ground dead, and the dragon laughed long and loud.

"What a wonderful day," he said. "I have won a human heart for free."

Satisfied, the dragon took the heart and crawled back down into his well. There he sat for a long time in the dark thinking how wonderful the heart would taste for dinner. He planned to eat it just as soon as it stopped beating. He planned to have it with potatoes and maybe a bottle of wine. The dragon got all excited imagining the wonderful feast he would have.

The only trouble was that after many days, the heart still hadn't stopped beating. Indeed, the sound of it pounding in the cold dark began to disturb the dragon. Because—as is well known—dragons have very sensitive ears. It got so the dragon couldn't even sleep, and he grew dizzy and bad-tempered. Yet never for a minute did he think of throwing the heart away. His hunger for it was too immense.

Finally, though, seven days after killing the girl, the dragon's hunger and fatigue grew so great that he could bear it no longer. Lifting the girl's heart in his scaly claws, he stuffed it in his mouth and swallowed it whole. For a moment he was satisfied; it had tasted good going down. But then he realized the heart was still beating inside him, and that scared him. Because, besides having very sensitive ears, dragons have no hearts. He didn't know what to do now that he had one. He didn't know how to get it out of him. He only knew that it was driving him crazy, the sound of it, pounding and pounding, even when he closed his eyes and pressed his claws over his ears and tried to rest.

"Oh," he moaned. "Poor me."

For another seven days the dragon wandered helplessly at the bottom of the well, banging his lizard head on the stone walls in frustration. Finally he called out for someone to help him—this monster that had never turned for help to anyone. At that moment he heard the girl's voice in his mind.

"What do you want?" she asked.

He stopped his pacing. "Who's there?"

"The girl whose heart you stole."

"It can't be. You're dead."

She ignored his remark. "You called out. What do you want?"

"Your heart—it's driving me crazy. I want you to take it away."

"You stole my heart, which contained all my sorrow and all my happiness. Yet you gave me nothing in return. Why should I help you?"

The dragon wept, another thing it had never done before. "Please. I will do anything you ask if you will just take it away."

"Are you sure? Anything?"

"Yes! Just get rid of it!"

"All right," the girl said. "But I have one condition. You must keep your end of your bargain first. You must give me your head."

The dragon was afraid. "But then I will die."

"Maybe. But you said you would give up anything for me to take it away. You are bound by your word, as you bound all the people who came to you before me."

The dragon was terrified. "But I have lived for centuries. I don't want to die."

"Then I can't help you," the girl said. "Goodbye."

"Wait!" the dragon called. "Come back! You have to help me!"

But the girl was gone. Yet her heart remained, pounding inside the dragon's chest, and with her departure, there was no hope for him ever to rest, ever to have a moment's peace. And, because of the heart he now possessed, the dragon knew that. He realized that it was *he* who had been tricked. That the only thing that would make the girl happy would be to slay him, and that she had done so even though it had cost her her very life.

"Damn you," the dragon said.

Picking up his sword, the dragon fell on it and cut off his own head.

The dragon died. Yet the girl's heart happily lived on. . . .

Beholding the Orion commander, Sarteen remembered her grandmother's story, and finally understood what it meant, for her, at least for her own soul. She turned to Pareen and smiled.

"I love you," she said.

Pareen smiled. "I love you."

Sarteen nodded in the direction of the alien invader, who stood poised with a sharp purple weapon pointed at her chest. "Welcome, Captain Eworl. I am Sarteen, commander of the starship *Crystal*. This is my first officer, Pareen." Then, gesturing in the direction of the communication board, where the nanoegg was hidden, she added, "And there's the ghost of my daughter. Do you see her? Do you recognize her? You met her once, a few hours ago, when you destroyed her world." Sarteen took a defiant step toward the enemy. "Do you remember her? You goddam dragon! Her name's . . . *Cira!*"

The human starship, *Crystal*, exploded, as did the alien vessel, *Adharma*.

Cool story. Both of them, all of them.

I am finished.

Except there is someone I must see. Someone I must say goodbye to. Perhaps, after I see her, I will not have a chance to make a final entry. My head pain weighs on me like ancient burdens. A last few concluding paragraphs should be no problem for me, however, even from a ghostly distance. I believe I do have a muse who helps me with my stories, an angel who watches over my life. In the same way, I have played my brother's muse before, when I dictated *Remember Me* to him. Perhaps I will play his muse one more time.

* * *

My old house, in Huntington Beach, is not entirely dark as I park out front. There is a light on in the kitchen. Someone is up late, probably unable to sleep. As I walk to the door, I wonder if this someone is sipping warm milk and thinking of me. I knock lightly, making it sound like the wind brushing against the wood. I do not wish to startle her. Yet my mother is quick to answer.

My mother bore my father scant resemblance, except that she was also attractive. She was tall and sleek, quick and loose. Her wide, thick-lipped mouth and her immaculately conceived black hair were her prizes.

Standing in her wrinkled bathrobe, she looks frail and tired, as if it has been a long time since she won a beauty prize.

"May I help you?" she asks.

"My name is Jean Rodrigues. I am the author of *Remember Me*. I am a friend of your son, Jimmy's. He told me you wanted to talk to me."

"Jim told you that?"

"Sort of. He said you had read my book."

"It's late. Why are you here?"

I shrug. "Honestly, I don't know, Mrs. Cooper."

She stares at me a long time and then steps aside. "Please come in."

We end up in the kitchen, where I came a few minutes after waking from my fatal fall. Then, *four* years ago, my mother and father sat around the table smoking and eating cake and talking about me as if I wasn't even there. Of course, they didn't know I was there. I was a ghost, invisible. Studying my mother across the table, I wonder if she knows now.

"Can I get you anything?" she asks.

I shake my head. "I'm fine, thank you."

She grips her glass of warm milk with both hands and stares into it as if it were a crystal ball. She has trouble looking at me. I understand. I appear completely different, but a part of her recognizes me *through* my eyes, the windows of my soul. Yet I will have to part the curtains on those windows if she is to see all the way inside. And I don't know if I want to do that.

"So," she begins. "You're the famous writer."

"Yes."

She nods. "I did read your book—*Remember Me.*" Her lower lip trembles. "It was a very good book. It touched me."

"Thank you," I say.

She glances up uneasily. "How long did it take you to write?"

"Not long. It came to me all at once, like a movie playing on a screen."

The questions are hard for her. She wants the truth but, like the rest of us, she knows intuitively it is too much for her. "Did something in particular inspire the story?"

"Yes."

She swallows. "Can you tell me what it was?"

"Your daughter."

"I see." She shudders. "Did you know Shari? Is

236

that why you adopted her name for your pen name?"

"Yes, I knew her. Better than anybody. She wanted me to write her story and I did." I hold up my hand as she starts to interrupt. "Please don't ask me where I knew her from. I can't tell you, and I'm sorry. Just know that her story is true and that she is fine. I know that above all else she would want you to know that."

Tears appear on my mother's face. "I don't understand."

I reach across the table and take her hand. "She goes on, we all go on. That's the point of the story. And wherever she is I know she would want me to tell you how much she loved you. That may not have come out as clearly as it should have in the story, but it's true. You were a great mother to her."

She sobs, shaking. "Who are you?"

"I'm a friend." I let go of her and sit back and put my hand to my head. A wave of severe pain rolls over me and I have trouble seeing. For a moment the world goes completely black and I have to strain to maintain consciousness. Forcing in a breath, I whisper, "I'm no one."

"Are you all right?" my mother asks, concerned.

I speak with effort. "I had a head injury. Sometimes it acts up and I get dizzy. Then I just have to lie down."

My mother stands and gently takes my arm. "Come, why don't you lie down in the living room."

I can barely get to my feet. "Thank you."

My mother is anxious. "Oh dear, you're as white as a ghost. Maybe you should lie down upstairs, in my daughter's old bedroom. I'll call for a doctor."

I smile faintly. "That's not necessary. I'll feel better in a few minutes. Just let me rest in her room. That's all I need." I pat her hand as she leads me toward the stairs. "Don't worry about me, really. This headache thing is nothing. It's so nice for me to be here with you."

"The world is a place to visit, to enjoy. It is not your permanent residence. When you don't know what to do, you return to your true home."

"It was nice of you to come to see me," she says with feeling.

My bed is freshly made. I sit down on the edge and my mother removes my shoes. Lying back, I feel the familiar comfort of a small child as she tucks a blanket over me. She leans over and I am surprised when she kisses me on the forehead.

"I feel like I know you," she says.

I brush her cheek with my hand, wipe away another tear that has come. How much I had prayed to do that for her in the days after I died. "You do know me," I say. "You remember me."

She doesn't fully understand but that is OK. After squeezing my hand and telling me to rest, she leaves the room, carefully closing the door behind her. In the same way I close my eyes. I know I will not open them again.

My peace is a divine gift, my joy a wonderful miracle. As I listen to my breathing slowly begin to run down, I remember how the last time I left I wished that I could have made my mark on the world, done something that would have changed the course of history. Something to be remembered by. Now I don't care about those things. I have been given the chance and done my best. No one waits on the other side to judge me. Besides, it doesn't really matter. It's all a play. God is not impressed by our acts, only by how much we love. I don't have to be important. I am grass, no one. Perhaps, in another place and time, I will learn the last of the yogi's lesson, and complete the flow of life.

I will become everyone.

EPILOGUE

*P*ETER NICHOLS AND JIMMY COOPER gathered in Jimmy's bedroom two hours after the funeral for Jean Rodrigues, bestselling author of numerous teenage thrillers and aspiring moviemaker. Jimmy sat at his desk in front of his computer, Peter on the edge of Jimmy's bed. From his back pocket, Peter withdrew a small square floppy disk and handed it to Jimmy.

"She was almost done with it when she went to see your mother," Peter said.

Jimmy nodded, studying the disk. "She wrote this during the last week?"

"Yes."

"How could she when she was in so much pain?"

Peter shrugged. "Writing always made her feel better. It was her first love."

Jimmy sadly shook his head. "You were her first love."

Peter nodded. "We both were." He bowed his head and a single tear slid down his cheek. He had not wept at the funeral, nor had Jimmy. There seemed no point; Shari would have just laughed at them. Yet the loss was hard for both of them, very hard. Peter added, "I can't believe how much she did in such a short time."

"Yeah. She was great." Jimmy's voice fell to a whisper as he remembered the end of her most important story. "She was the best sister a guy could've had."

Peter sighed and stood. "I have to go. There are things that have to be wrapped up right away."

Jimmy also stood. "I understand. How's your back?"

"Perfect. Not even a twinge."

"That's amazing."

"It's a miracle." Peter patted him on the shoulder. "Take care of yourself."

"You, too." Jimmy hugged him. "Will you be all right?"

Peter sniffed. "Yeah. It'll take time, but I'll be fine. I have my work to do."

"Coaching?"

Peter nodded. "There's that—I won't quit helping the kids. But Shari left me a pile of money. Now I'll be able to do more. The Rishi and the yogi said to serve. I want to try to help the Hispanic community in the inner cities somehow."

"Good for you. I saw Shari's will. She left her Hispanic family a tidy sum as well. Not that I'm complaining—she left me far more than I deserved. I never knew she was so rich."

Peter was sad. "She was rich in many ways." He touched Jimmy's arm. "Let's stay in touch, OK?"

"Sure. We'll talk tomorrow."

"Good." Peter paused as he stepped toward the door, and glanced at the computer. "Are you sure you'll be able to finish her story?"

"She once dictated a whole book to me, and after she returned to Earth, we were closer than ever. I don't think there will be any problem."

Peter smiled faintly. "It will probably be another best-seller."

"I'm sure that would have made her laugh."

"Goodbye, Jimmy."

"Goodbye, Peter."

After Peter was gone, Jimmy turned on his computer and loaded the floppy disk into his word processor. For the next four hours he read his sister's last story, and when he came to the part where she went to see his mother, he briefly closed his eyes and prayed for guidance. He was not praying long when a tap on his shoulder made him jump. He opened his eyes and whirled around.

But, of course, the room was empty.

Jimmy smiled. "All right, I'll start writing. If I make a mistake, we can always fix it in galleys."

Rolling up his sleeves, Jimmy began to type. This time he was awake and knew he wasn't dreaming. Her funeral had been nothing more than a social obligation he had to attend. His sister was alive. He would see her again someday. They would meet in a place of light and splendor and both would remember today and yesterday and days so long ago their history could only be found in forgotten ancient myths, such as "The Starlight Crystal."

About the Author

CHRISTOPHER PIKE was born in Brooklyn, New York, but grew up in Los Angeles, where he lives to this day. Prior to becoming a writer, he worked in a factory, painted houses, and programmed computers. His hobbies include astronomy, meditating, running, playing with his nieces and nephews, and making sure his books are prominently displayed in local bookstores. He is the author of *Last Act, Spellbound, Gimme a Kiss, Remember Me, Scavenger Hunt, Final Friends* 1, 2, and 3, *Fall into Darkness, See You Later, Witch, Die Softly, Bury Me Deep, Whisper of Death, Chain Letter 2: The Ancient Evil, Master of Murder, Monster, Road to Nowhere, The Eternal Enemy, The Immortal, The Wicked Heart, The Midnight Club, The Last Vampire, The Last Vampire 2: Black Blood,* and *Remember Me 2: The Return,* all available from Archway Paperbacks. *Slumber Party, Weekend, Chain Letter,* and *Sati*—an adult novel about a very unusual lady—are also by Mr. Pike.